GILL

EastEnders' Great Love Story

GILL AND MARK

EastEnders' Great Love Story

by
Susanna Dawson

Illustrated by David Haldane

RED FOX

A Red Fox Book
Published by Random House Children's Books
20 Vauxhall Bridge Road, London SW1V 2SA2

A division of Random House UK Ltd
London Melbourne Sydney Auckland
Johannesburg and agencies throughout the world

First published in 1993 by Red Fox

Set in Garamond Roman by Deltatype Ltd, Ellesmere Port, Cheshire
Printed and bound in Great Britain
by Cox & Wyman Ltd, Reading, Berkshire

RANDOM HOUSE UK Limited Reg. No. 954009

ISBN 0 09 9318415

CONTENTS

INTRODUCTION

I'm Susanna Dawson and I played GILL ROBIN-SON in EASTENDERS, the girl who married Mark Fowler and died of HIV-related illness.

Gill's death in EASTENDERS was watched by over 20 million people, that's getting on for half the population of Great Britain. I received over 2000 letters from the public, and even now I'm still replying to them!

It's these experiences that have made me want to write this book. Playing the role of Gill Robinson in EASTENDERS changed my thinking about HIV.

If you take risks and become HIV+ your life will change forever.

It's an issue we all have to face, and face now.

Take care of yourself and other people, and, where you can, pass the word around.

There's a video available of The Gill and Mark Story, with interviews from the EASTENDERS cast, people affected by HIV and young people talking about the issue.

Buy it and you'll be helping support people with HIV and AIDS – see p. 13 for details of how to get it.

ACKNOWLEDGMENTS

My name is on the cover of this book, but that's only half the story. Throughout the Gill and Mark book and video project we have had invaluable assistance and support from our specialist panel, who have given time and expert advice, providing resources and helping to make our information as relevant, up to date and accurate as possible.

Elaine Darbyshire	of the National Union of Teachers
Gill Lenderyou	of the Family Planning Association and Brook Advisory Centres
Leonard Lewis	Executive Producer EASTENDERS BBC TV
Rita O'Brien	North East Thames Regional Health Authority
Huw Meredith & Ian Poitier	National Aids Trust
Viv Pound	PSE Teacher, Norfolk LEA
John Seex	Peer co-ordinators Condom Project
Sali Walker	Tower Hamlets Health Authority
Rashida Sharif	PSE adviser Birmingham Education Dept
John Shine	Senior Nurse Counsellor Red Admiral Project
Rachel Thomson	Sex Education Forum
Roger Tyrrell	Head of Communicable Diseases Unit, Department of Health
Danielle Wayne	Education Officer, Health Education Authority

The author and the publishers of the book gratefully acknowledge permission from the BBC and EastEnders unit to use material, characters and storylines from the series.

The publishers are grateful to the British Medical Association for kind permission to use illustrations within this book reprinted from their publication *Aids and You: An Illustrated Guide to HIV and AIDS (1992)*.

My special thanks to:
Dr Rak Nandwani MB BS MRCP MRC Research Fellow Registrar in HIV medicine, Chelsea and Westminster Hospital. Doctor and friend to clients with HIV. For checking and rewording endless drafts.

David Haldane – who has done all the fab cartoons throughout the book, and Caroline, my editor, for being so supportive.

Mervyn Watson (Deputy Head Series Drama BBC TV), Tony McHale (Story Consultant EastEnders), Lilie Ferrari (Script Editor), Brendan Cassin, Deborah Cook, Susan Boyd (writers) and of course Carolyn in the production office.

Russell, Michael Cashman, Joanne, Sarah, Steve, Denise, Adam, Anna, Paul, Mark, Sheila, Malcolm, Andria who have all contributed with pieces from their own lives and who have been brave enough to stand up and be counted.

BHAN, Catholic Aids link, 'Stepping Out', Christine and Andy at the Hungerford Drugs Project, Nicola Smith, Patrick Gayle and Dennis Gray.

Martin at Positively Irish Action on AIDS
Rob and the Bloomsbury Community Care Team
Hazel Yabsley and all at Positive Youth

Crusaid who have supported our project and fight to raise awareness

Simon Whatney for being so angry about the spread of this disease and how it affects us, and for fighting every day to stop it.

Jeremy Joseph, for giving people a voice, for trying to change things for the better.

Todd Carty, Sue Tully, Jacquetta May and Colin Kerrigan who have backed me from Day One.

The Princess of Wales for her unceasing support and care of people living with HIV. She has done more than anyone to try and stop the prejudice.

Chris, Mum, Dad and Alison who have stuck by me and without whom I could never have brought up Joe and continued working.

And lastly, Tim, to whom this book is dedicated, godfather to Joe and forever friend to me.

This book is endorsed by Crusaid and the National AIDS Trust

Chapter 1
GILL'S STORY

6th March

Went out to the club last night with Tina and the crowd. And for once, things turned out a bit different from the usual scampi and chips . . .

It was around half past ten and Tina was holding court as usual when this guy comes past our table with a pint in his hand. Well, Tina sticks her leg out and she trips him up. Everyone laughed, but it wasn't funny really, half the beer went over me, and I got soaked.

He was ever so embarrassed, kept offering to mop it up with this soggy old bit of tissue, making it worse of course. And all the girls were laughing and saying, 'Go for it, Gill!' stuff like that. I was dead embarrassed. Didn't know where to put my face, I kept giggling and feeling sorry for him at the same time.

I kind of knew he was nice too, but there's no way I could let on. I could kill 'em sometimes.

Anyway, through all this, he says he's never been to the club before and that he was a friend of Barry's.

He's not from round here; London, he said, but he's renting a room in a flat in Andover Street.

Enough of all that. He asked for my phone

number, sort of mumbled it, but the thing was, how do I give it him without all the girls catching on?

He seems really nice, it's not like me to go for a guy just like that, but he seems different somehow, and he didn't try it on; maybe that's what it was.

Well, I gave it to him anyway, the number that is, but he didn't have anything to write it down with, so he said he'd repeat it to himself, over and over, till he got a pencil.

Don't know what I think really, stupid actually, I only saw the bloke for 5 minutes and it was dark.

Anyway, I don't know why I'm bothering, he probably won't even ring....

Hope he does though....

25th March

God, funny to think that was only three weeks ago. I feel as if I've known Mark for years.

The week after that we went out three times and since then ... well, we've seen each other practically every day since.

Tina's complaining; says I'm going to lose all my real friends and when he ditches me I'll be really lonely.

Great having mates like that, isn't it?

Still, I sort of know what she means.

You know, I can't bear the thought of him going off me. There's something about him, he's really not like other guys. . . . he doesn't have to keep proving stuff all the time, going on about how fantastic he is, things like that.

The one thing that worries me though, is that he doesn't seem to have many friends and he won't tell me anything about his family and why he came up here.

I can't make him out really.

2nd May

We had a row about 'it' today.

You know, it's not that I don't want to, it's just that it's really stupid to take risks like that.

I don't know what the chances are of getting pregnant if you don't use anything but it'd just be my kind of luck if that happened to me.

Probably first time as well.

I think it depends on where you are in the month, but I have to say is it worth it?

I know guys don't think like that but then they aren't the ones it happens to. I mean, can you imagine having a baby now, just when everything's looking so good, when the job's going well and I've found a place to live?

You couldn't go out when you wanted, you'd never be able to afford new clothes and stuff, and would he stay?

Something tells me that he'd be off like a shot.

'Course, I suppose you could always go for an abortion, but that's really scary.

Remember Sarah, what she went through?

First it took her weeks to admit it to herself, then it was almost too late for her to have it done on the National Health and then, on top of all that she got an infection which went on for more than three weeks!

And of course, she had to tell her parents.

The very thought of it sends me cold.

'Course the whole school found out, nobody stuck by her, everyone called her a slag, wouldn't sit next to her and all that.

And if we're being really truthful here, I wasn't too nice either, making sure I didn't get to be on my own with her.

And how long did that go on?

Well, right up until Ronnie Bryce nicked that stuff from the Head's office and got suspended, and we all had something new to talk about.

I know that's a long time back, all that, but god, I couldn't go through it.

I dunno, I don't know what I'm saying really, maybe all this stuff is just an excuse in my head, maybe it's because I don't know if I want to sleep with him right now or not.

One of my problems is sorting out whether it's to do with the fact that I'm not on the Pill at the moment or whether I want to lose another two pounds off my tummy before he sees me in the altogether!

Stupid, isn't it?

11th May

Guess what?

WAIT FOR IT. . . . We did it!

It all started at half past six last Saturday evening.

Mark and I had this stupid row about a can of baked beans; would you believe it!

What happened was this: I was doing his tea and he was telling me off; he kept going on and on about how I never listen to him and I just go off and make arrangements for things he doesn't want to do.

This was all because I'd told Jackie we'd go bowling with the crowd on Sunday night and I hadn't asked him first.

It's not true of course.

I always ask him, I just forgot to this time and I knew he'd want to come anyway.

Well, it turns out he didn't.

What I'm trying to say, I suppose, is that in the middle of all this, he picks up this can of beans and charges into the lounge ranting and raving.

Well, the beans were a bit open so as he's going on, waving them about in the air, bits of the sauce started splashing out, going all over the sofa.

I started laughing; he said it wasn't funny; so I said, couldn't he take a joke, and picked up this tin of pineapple pieces. . . .

Well, he went mad, didn't he, and went to grab me. . . .

And then. . . .

Well, what can I say?

He gets me but instead of going for me he starts kissing me doesn't he, and well, I suppose what I'm trying to say is that we ended up doing it.

On the kitchen floor.

Sounds romantic, doesn't it?

In fact, it wasn't that good; the earth didn't exactly move, but we did have a laugh.

All I was worried about was whether someone would come in or not and that my bum was getting burnt by the electric fire. Of course, I was too embarrassed to tell him that, or to ask him to move a bit further away.

I think I'm falling in love with him.

30th May

I haven't written for ages because I've been really worried. After all I said as well.

The thing is, I didn't come on for what seemed like months. I was two and a half weeks late and I'm usually dead regular. So you can imagine what I was going through.

And the funny thing is that when I did, eventually, I felt a bit sad, suddenly I got all broody about babies and stuff.

Not for long though, I'm relieved now, I can tell you that. When you think back it was so stupid to take that kind of risk, we weren't even drunk.

I always thought I was a bit more grown up than that. I feel quite ashamed really.

Still, there's no use crying over spilt milk. I've made an appointment at the family planning and I'm telling you, it's the Pill for me from now on.

I'm not going to go through that again, I have never been so worried in all my life.

June 2nd

Had to leave work early today to get to the clinic on time. Apparently because of the cuts our clinic is only open from 2–4 on Mondays and Wednesdays, and as I'm not registered with a GP up here I couldn't go to my doctor.

Had to tell the boss that I was going to the dentist, then of course he asked to see the card, didn't he!

I said I'd lost it, he didn't believe me and now he says he's going to dock my pay.

Miserable old sod.

Anyway, they were really nice at the clinic, put me on a low dose one: all that means is you have to take it at the same time every day and you take it all through the month even when you're on.

The lady asked me if I wanted any condoms, which I must say I thought was a bit weird, seeing as she'd just given me the Pill.

But then she said that I wouldn't be safe for the first month and she started going on about AIDS.

Typical doctor, I suppose she's got to say that because it's in the papers such a lot, but I had to laugh.

What was really good though was that there were lots of blokes there.

I asked Mark if he'd come with me but he said he was too embarrassed, but there was almost as many guys as girls and not all of them were in couples either.

And no one looked.

You just get your number called out, they don't use your name.

Next time he can jolly well come with me.

So I'm safe now.

I feel one whole lot better, I can tell you.

June 3rd

Going on the Pill has really made me think.

I feel strange somehow, like it's a kind of commitment to Mark, saying we want to be together.

Not that I'd sleep with anyone else, anyway, but still it feels different.

I'm a bit scared of it all, it seems to be happening much too quick and I don't know if I'm ready.

Ready for what?

I don't know, he hasn't suggested anything like that, so I don't know what I'm fussing for.

HIV/AIDS – THE BASIC FACTS

When it comes to sex all kinds of things can happen: things you want to happen – things you don't!

Perhaps the last thing that's going through your head is whether it's 'safe' or not!

Confused? So were they! Gill and Mark got it wrong in every kind of way:

★ Gill didn't think she was ready for sex at that time.

★ They weren't using contraception against pregnancy.

★ They weren't protecting themselves or each other against HIV and other STDs (Sexually Transmitted Diseases), ie. they weren't using CONDOMS.

So, in a word, what's it all about?

AIDS is caused by a tiny virus called HIV. It leaves you vulnerable to serious diseases which can be fatal.

THERE IS NO KNOWN CURE FOR HIV.

Who's at risk?
Anyone and everyone that takes part in sexual behaviour or shares needles runs the risk of getting HIV.

That's all of us: black, white, pink or brown, old, young, fat, thin. You, me, your family, your mates, gay, straight, bisexual. . . . you name it, we're all at risk.

The virus can't tell what country it's in, or which body or liquid, it doesn't know the difference between people, and it has no prejudice. This little bug is happy to play with all of us; it doesn't want to leave anyone out!

Gill didn't think it was her problem, nobody ever does, but it could affect anybody, and it's spreading fast.

●●●●●●●●●●●●●●●●●●●●●●●●●●●●●●●●●●●●●●●

FACT: In 1989 there were 117,499 teenage pregnancies in Britain
In 1992 it was 120,000
98% of these were the result of sex without a condom.

●●●●●●●●●●●●●●●●●●●●●●●●●●●●●●●●●●●●●●●

HOW DO YOU GET IT?

This virus can be passed on if infected bodily fluids from another person (their blood or semen or vaginal fluids) get into YOUR bloodstream. The most likely ways for this to happen are:

★ Having unprotected, penetrative sex with someone who has the virus (that's homosexual OR heterosexual sex where a penis enters the body, either into the vagina or the anus), even if it doesn't end in orgasm.

★ Using a syringe which has been used by someone who has the virus. This means you're sticking THEIR infected blood into YOUR arm or leg.

This doesn't happen in a dentist's, doctor's or hospital, but many, many drug users have been infected by sharing needles (often called 'works').

The virus can occasionally be passed from the mother to the unborn child: in the womb, through breastmilk or during childbirth.

WHAT'S SAFE AND WHAT'S NOT

YOU CAN'T GET HIV FROM:

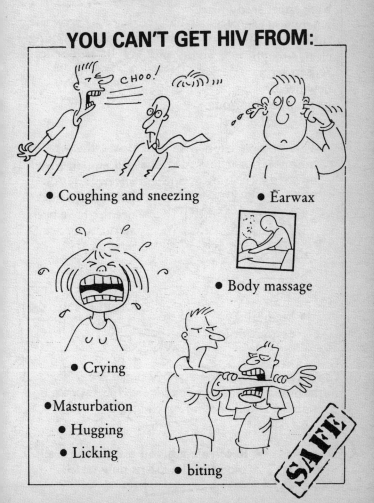

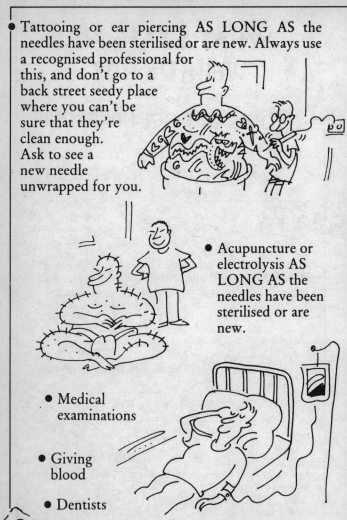

- Tattooing or ear piercing AS LONG AS the needles have been sterilised or are new. Always use a recognised professional for this, and don't go to a back street seedy place where you can't be sure that they're clean enough. Ask to see a new needle unwrapped for you.

- Acupuncture or electrolysis AS LONG AS the needles have been sterilised or are new.

- Medical examinations

- Giving blood

- Dentists

- Receiving a blood transfusion – all blood in the UK is now tested

SAFE

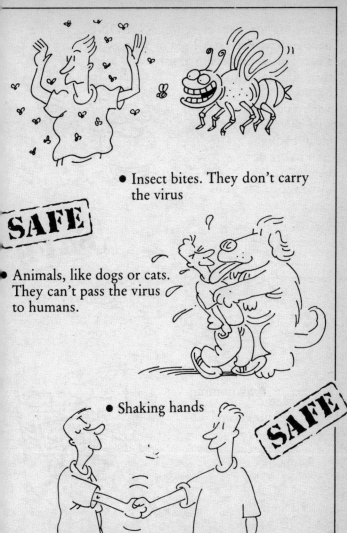

- Insect bites. They don't carry the virus

SAFE

- Animals, like dogs or cats. They can't pass the virus to humans.

- Shaking hands

SAFE

- Kissing

SAFE

- Swimming

- Sharing the same toilet seat

• Sharing bed clothes

• Sharing a house, flat, school, or workplace.

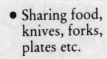

• Sharing food, knives, forks, plates etc.

TAKE CARE! RISKY!

Tattooing other people and yourself or piercing ears or other parts of the body is not too hot an idea. The sharp equipment may be dirty and you could transfer tiny particles of blood from one person into another.

Cutting yourself to mix blood, as in becoming blood brothers is not good news, too risky.

LOW RISK

Oral sex, that's licking or sucking your partner's genitals, is reckoned to be a LOW RISK ACTIVITY, which means safer than penetrative sex but not totally safe. It might be unsafe, especially if you have mouth infections like herpes or mouth ulcers. To be really safe, you should use a condom – try flavoured ones.

Fingering/heavy petting: that's putting your fingers into your partner's vagina or anus is SAFE as long as you don't cut the skin or have any open cuts or sores on your hands.

★ LOVE BITES ★ ★ LOVE BITES ★

Are they safe? Well, pretty safe, yeah, as long as you've not got open sores in your mouth and you don't cut the skin.

● ●

FACT: 1 in 5 young women (16–21yrs) has had sex with 4 or more partners.

● ●

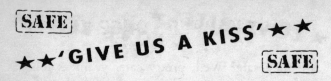

Kissing is lovely, it makes you feel good and warm and it's safe. Nobody's ever contracted or passed on HIV through a kiss!

●●●●●●●●●●●●●●●●●●●●●●●●●●●●●●●●●●

FACT: Nearly 30% of young men claim to have 3 or more partners in a year.

●●●●●●●●●●●●●●●●●●●●●●●●●●●●●●●●●●

WHAT HAPPENS ONCE YOU'VE GOT HIV?

Once you're HIV+ the current thinking says that within a period of time you will go on to contract an HIV related illness (ie. one of those illnesses that gets into your system because your body's defences are low – pneumonia is a common one). Once you have one of the HIV related illnesses, then, at the moment, your condition is given a new name – you're considered to have AIDS.

AIDS is not just a single illness that you can die of. It's the virus living inside your body and destroying the body's fighter cells, making it easy for other diseases to get right on in there and weaken your body so much that in the end one of them may kill you . . .

Half the people who get the HI virus are entirely well ten years after they first got it. Many of these people remain alive for up to five years more. The other half suffer from a variety of illnesses and infections. At the moment, people don't seem to live much beyond 15 years once they're HIV+.

HOWEVER . . .

Don't panic about all this. HIV isn't going to jump you from out of the air. The virus is really quite a fragile little thing and doesn't survive long outside the body. And normal everyday bodily contact is NOT going to get you infected – remember the virus has to get into your bloodstream.

WHAT DO ALL THESE LETTERS STAND FOR ANYWAY?

HIV stands for HUMAN IMMUNO-DEFICIENCY VIRUS. It's a virus that attacks your immune system, which are the sort of blood cells that prevent you getting seriously ill from all the illnesses around.

AIDS stands for ACQUIRED IMMUNO-DEFICIENCY SYNDROME. So that says much the same thing – it means your body has developed a syndrome (set of symptoms) which show that you haven't got enough disease-fighting blood cells to cope with illnesses and infection.

● ●

FACT: 9% of HIV cases are aged between 15 and 19 in Scotland (at the end of '92).

● ●

HIV– Stands for HIV negative, ie. someone who hasn't been infected with the virus.

 HIV+ Stands for HIV positive, ie. someone who has been infected with the virus and can infect other people but who hasn't yet fallen seriously ill (which would lead to an AIDS diagnosis).

PWA Stands for Person With AIDS. Someone who is living with an AIDS diagnosis.

AIDS SCOREBOARD	
People with AIDS	
1981	*1*
1987 FEB	*731*
1990 DEC	*4098*
1993	*11.500 ?*

VERY IMPORTANT – FREE UP YOUR ATTITUDE

HIV and AIDS

The word AIDS has a lot of unpleasant things associated with it. The newspapers scream AIDS VICTIMS!!! AIDS TERROR!!! AIDS KILLERS!!!

People talk about AIDS with fear and hate and prejudice quite unlike that talked about with any other illness.

Why is it?

I reckon it's because it's about our three great taboos: SEX, DISEASE and DEATH!

And the British, with the good old 'stiff upper lip' and all that, are just great at brushing these 'nasties' under the carpet.

It doesn't make them go away though, does it?

We've got to look at WHAT IS, not what people would like it to be, and act on that.

Firstly, the important thing is to TAKE CARE OF YOURSELF AND WHAT YOU DO.

Secondly (this is more general), it's important to do what you can to CHANGE OPINIONS and free up your attitudes a little.

Let's try and stop this prejudice and start by getting rid of the word 'AIDS'.

For people living with HIV it can be pretty earth-shattering to get that positive diagnosis. What's the point of making them go through all the trauma a second time when diagnosed AIDS?

The word can spell fear for people who are positive and it allows people who are negative to see it as someone else's problem.

None of this helps any of us to stay well, relaxed and happy.

Isn't just saying HIV+ enough? That's what we're going to do in this book, and what many people would like to see happen. So what we're going to call it from now on is HIV illness or HIV-related illness.

In this book where others might use the word AIDS, we'll put it in brackets.

● ●

FACT: Recent improvements in condom use are most evident among 21–24 year olds and 16–17 year olds. (That's one in the eye for the wrinklies! Sue.)

● ●

QUESTIONS AND ANSWERS ABOUT SEX

I love this guy, Mike, but I don't know if I should do it or not?
If you're uncertain it's probably best not to.

There's not much fun if you have sex for any other reason than that you both care for each other and want to make that commitment.

Having sex is pretty pointless otherwise and can be risky without the right protection.

Best to wait.

● ●

FACT: Amongst men who had two or more sexual partners in the last year, 44% hadn't used a condom within the last three months. (That means they're having unsafe sex! Sue.)

THERE ARE TWO KINDS OF BOY.
ONE WHO USES A CONDOM WHEN HAVING SEX AND ONE WHO JUST TALKS ABOUT USING A CONDOM WHEN HAVING SEX

● ●

SOME GREAT REASONS NOT TO HAVE SEX:

☆ *I'm not using/haven't got any contraceptives at the moment so I might get pregnant*

☆ *I don't want to have sex just because everyone else is doing it. I want to wait a bit.*

☆ *My parents/friends might turn up/come in. I don't want them to know what we're doing.*

☆ *We've had a lot to drink, I want us to make love when we know what we're doing.*

☆ *I'm into celibacy, I think you can have a more intense relationship that way.*

☆ *I'm having my period (I'm on at the moment).*

☆ *We haven't any condoms, so we'll be at risk of passing on something, like HIV.*

☆ *I'm still a virgin. I feel too nervous about this/I want to stay that way.*

☆ *I'm under 16 and it's against the law. You might be prosecuted if we're caught.*

☆ *It's against my religion.*

☆ *I respect myself too much.*

☆ *I'm in control of my own body, and at the moment that's not what I want.*

☆ *I'm worried I might feel guilty. I always tell my mum everything.*

How do I know when I'm ready?
Do you mean to have sex?

This answer is going to sound like a cop out but you aren't ready until you do know!

The first time can always be delayed and I reckon it should *be until it's the right person.*

My first sexual encounter was horrible. It was with this guy called Paul who was one of our group but who I wasn't going out with.

I'd just been dumped by this bloke who I'd been seeing for over a year.

I hadn't had sex with him but we had been very serious and I was missing him a lot.

I thought I'd try and forget him by getting off with Paul, and for some reason we ended up in his parent's bedroom, and we did it.

I had got into this situation where we were kissing and stuff and because he was older than me and everybody else fancied him I was too embarrassed to say no.

It was horrible. I ended up hurting and it didn't feel good at all.

We then spent the whole of the rest of the afternoon washing and ironing to get the sheets clean before his Mum and Dad came back!

If I'd had the courage to say no, I would have felt a whole lot better.

FOR WHERE TO GET A CONDOM AND HOW TO PUT IT ON – SEE CHAPTER TWO

●●●●●●●●●●●●●●●●●●●●●●●●●●●●●

FACT: 70% of 16–20-year-olds are having sexual
relationships and they are more likely to
have numerous partners than the general
adult population. (That means young people bonk more people than their parents.
Surprise! Sue.)

●●●●●●●●●●●●●●●●●●●●●●●●●●●●

**I don't really want to have sex with my boyfriend
but I do want to be close and show how much I love
him.
So I suppose I should really, shouldn't I?**
*Sex isn't just penetrative. It's sharing all kinds of
physical, private experiences with someone else.*

There are loads of things to enjoy, it doesn't have to involve intercourse – like:

Kissing	✯ *On the lips or anywhere else.*
Body Rubbing	✯ *Touching and holding body against body – try a private dance session*
Fingering	✯ *Using your fingers to excite your partner. Stroke neck, temple, feet, elbows, the back of his knees.*
Dirty Talking	✯ *A real turn on and totally safe.*
Role Playing	✯ *Act out your fantasies!*
Sucking/Licking	✯ *Toes, ears . . . all over the body. French kissing is safe.*
Washing	✯ *Sharing shower/bath and washing each other.*
Hugging	✯ *Cuddling and holding.*
Massage	✯ *Use scented oils and take turns.*

FACT: In the UK, condom usage with a new partner remains a minority activity at 6%. (That means 94% are having unsafe sex! Sue.)

Chapter 2
GILL'S STORY

July 3rd

Can't believe the weather right now. Try typing in this heat, in our office — it's like a greenhouse or something.

We went up to the lido tonight, straight after work. It was still so warm we swam and mucked about till gone seven.

Then I met Mark at The Feathers for a drink.

He's embarrassed because he's never got any money. Makes me slip him a fiver so he can go to the bar.

I don't see it really, there's no big deal attached to being out of work, 'specially these days. It's happening to everyone, teachers and that, not just ordinary people.

Anyway, something will come up.

I quite like it in a way — gives me some power. Role reversal they call it!

July 6th

We talked about living together this evening!

Well, Mark did. I pretended I wasn't sure and went all cool on him.

Said I'd have to think about it.

'Course there isn't really much to think about, I love him to death and we'd save a load of money on my room.

He could still get the social to pay his rent and then all my money (all I say, as if it was some great amount!) could go on bills and having a good time; well, living anyway.

It'd be great, we wouldn't be quite as strapped as we are now.

And we're going really steady now; we've been together exactly four months today. In fact this is our ⅓rd anniversary!

Aug 10th

I can't believe it. I hate life right now. I'm in bed with cystitis.

Cystitis has got to be the pits! Your stomach aches non-stop, (thanks, Mum, for the rabbit hot water bottle) and I've got to keep my legs permanently crossed because I feel like weeing all the time!

You know what the cure's supposed to be? Black coffee and putting live yogurt up you! Smear it round a tampon, this article said.

I sent Mark out to get some, he comes back with a pot of Ski low-fat strawberry flavour!

Moaned when I made him go back into town to the health food place.

Doesn't seem to be doing much good, mind, it

really hurts when I wee and there's this smelly grungy stuff in my knickers.

God, it's disgusting, and it makes me feel really unclean.

I suppose if it gets much worse I shall have to go and see the doctor.

I don't want to, I get so embarrassed about stuff like that.

It's really hard to ask some grown man to poke about down there and then see him in the supermarket next week doing his groceries.

'Oh hello, Mr Singh' . . . and then me blushing 'cos I know where his finger's been.

I'll have to do something about it though, this is my third day off sick, and if you have more than that they dock your pay, 'less you have a doctor's certificate.

Oct 11th

Well, I got my sick note, he wrote it out for two weeks.

He asked me loads of questions: how long I'd been feeling like this? Whether I had any rashes on my skin? When did I have flu? How long have I had a discharge?

Then he took a sample.

It wasn't half as bad as I thought actually, the same as a smear test. He puts a cold metal thing up you and then takes a bit from inside with a wooden scraper sort of thing. It doesn't hurt you, you just feel a bit silly.

Gave me one of those stupid bottles to pee in.

Have you ever tried aiming into one of those? I tell you, it's useless!

I got wee all over my hands, the loo seat ... everywhere but in the bottle. All right for blokes, they can just aim and shoot. Full marks every time; I managed a centimetre!

By this time I could see the funny side of it, and I didn't mind what he did to me.

Of course, he said there was nothing to worry about, it was all routine. Needless to say, I'm worried.

Why do I always think the worst?

Someone my age couldn't have cancer. Could they?

There's a lot of cancer in our family. My mum always says she'll never make old bones.

But two weeks off work? There's got to be a reason. He said the laboratory they use was very good and we should have the results by the end of the week. Get the 'we', it's my body isn't it?

I don't know, I expect I'm imagining it but there was something in his voice.

Mark says I'm being stupid, worrying over nothing, and the sooner it's cleared up the better, then we can get back to it.

God, that's all they think about, isn't it?

Oct 13th

Well, the pills seem to be working. I'm only in the loo every half hour now and it's stopped hurting quite so much.

Seeing as I'm in there such a lot I thought I'd have a go at decorating the bathroom.

I'll keep to the yellow theme 'cos the suite's in lemon but instead of that yucky beige I thought it might be nice in a minty colour, sort of fresh, you know.

There's this one on the chart called 'sea view' which might look quite good – make it look nice and cool.

I'll ask Mark what he thinks tonight.

And then I thought I'd try this stencilling thing. There's this offer you can send for in the magazine. It's really good, you get the stuff – the stencils, the brushes and a 'step by step guide' on how to do it.

Don't see how you can go wrong really . . . it's got to be better than what we've got, anyway.

I thought the stencil could be in a slightly darker shade than the walls; not too much, just so it looks subtle, like proper wallpaper.

In the offer you can have fishes and seashells or flowers. They're the same price but it's only one or the other.

Oct 14th

Mark said he didn't mind what it was so I've gone for the seashells.

You've got to keep to the theme and in the end I thought flowers would be OK in a kitchen but they've not really got much to do with water, have they?

Oct 20th

Well, I went in the shop and got all the stuff I need. 'Course 'sea view' turns out to be one of those mixes doesn't it? In just about the most expensive range as well.

It's a real con – they don't do it in small sizes! You have to get it in five litres or more!

Well, there'd be masses left over and you couldn't do the whole flat in it.

But then I had a brainwave.

Instead of getting the two colours – you know, for the stencil bit in the next shade up, I thought why not just get a small can of ordinary white and then mix it in to what's left over?

That way you get your two colours but you don't pay twice the price!

Good, eh?

Anyway, that's what I've done.

Can't wait to get started.

Oct 22nd

Went into town today to get the rest of the stuff for the bathroom.

BHS do a lovely range and it's all matching.

I managed to find face flannels, towels and a shower curtain all with fishes printed on them. Not exactly printed but sort of moulded out of the material, if you know what I mean.

They look really good, because they're almost the same as the stencils on the walls.

I did loads in the end, going in a sort of line round the bath.

It wasn't quite as easy as I thought actually, one or two of them went a bit smudgy but it's not where you'd notice.

It looks really original.

And then in Boots I found these soaps like sea animals and stuff. So I've put them on the windowsill.

I think it looks good.

Can't wait for Mark to get home.

Oct 23rd

I think it looks brilliant.

He says it's like the inside of Finchley Road baths.

The man's got no taste.

FACTS ABOUT STD's

This stands for **SEXUALLY TRANSMITTED DIS-EASE** and I'm telling you, there's loads of the little bug. . . .s around.

You can get all or any of them by having sex without a condom.

And some of them hurt, some of them make you sterile (no babies), and some of them can kill.

I'll quickly run down this list and if you think 'yeuuch!' by the end of it you'll be right.

CHLAMYDIA   With this one, you get pain during sex, strange discharge, burning sensation when peeing. Can be cleared up with antibiotics but not nice.

GENITAL WARTS Small bumps grow on your vagina, penis or anus, sometimes in your throat. Quite often inside you so you don't always notice. Causes pain and some doctors believe they can be linked to cervical cancer. Treated by special stuff which destroys the root.

PID (PELVIC INFLAMMATORY DISEASE) Women get it and some don't even know. Can cause pain, heavy periods, chills, nausea and vomiting. Leads to pregnancy problems and can put your life at risk. Treated by antibiotics and sometimes an operation. You could end up sterile.

GONORRHOEA (The Clap) I thought this went out with the Ark but thousands still pass it on every year. Blokes usually get a pus-like discharge from their penis. Women often don't notice anything. It can make you sterile (no babies) and give you arthritis and heart disease. If you're pregnant it could kill the baby.

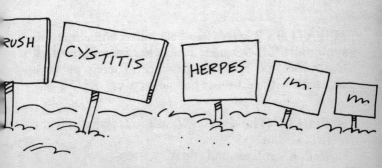

GENITAL HERPES   Like cold sores but on your genitals. Once you've got them they'll be back. For life. They're not curable and can be passed on to your partners.

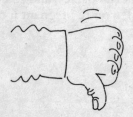

HEPATITIS B   This can be a killer. Sometimes no symptoms, other times, headaches, vomiting, dark frothy pee, no appetite, jaundice. There's no cure although with rest most people recover.

SYPHILIS (The Pox)   Wasn't this what Henry VIIIth died of?

Well, it's still around today.

Untreated it can cause blindness, mental illness, heart disease and death. Very infectious in the early stages.

NSU (NON SPECIFIC URETHRITIS) I've had this. You itch like mad and have a smelly discharge. It can be cleared up by antibiotics but that takes a long time.

■■■■■■■■■■■■■■■■■■■■■■■■■■■

The Common Market wanted to standardise condoms, making them all the same size. But the Italians objected, saying the smallest size of 55mm was too BIG for some of their willies!

■■■■■■■■■■■■■■■■■■■■■■■■■■■

YEUUCH!!!!!! ALL THESE CAN BE GOT FROM SEX WITHOUT A CONDOM. IS IT WORTH IT?

CRABS Little animals (about the size of dandruff, flattish and grey/white) that crawl around in your

pubic hair eating up the dead bits of skin and generally breeding. Not harmful but dead itchy. Can be killed by nit lotion.

Unfortunately these guys have learnt to jump over condoms, so if your partner's got crabs the likelihood is you'll get them too.

■■■■■■■■■■■■■■■■■■■■■■■■■■■■■■■■

MUSICAL CONDOM   There's a musical one which plays the Beatles LOVE ME DO when excitement hits fever pitch! (and we all know when that is!)

YOU HAD TO WEAR THE GUNS N' ROSES MUSICAL CONDOM, DIDN'T YOU?

■■■■■■■■■■■■■■■■■■■■■■■■■■■■■■■■

THRUSH   is an itchy mouth and
                          genital infection that is
                          NOT a sexually transmit-
                          ted disease.

CYSTITIS   isn't either, though it can be caused by friction as a result of sex.

HERPES   (that's cold sores) can be got through sex but that's not the only route.

HEPATITIS A   can be got from dirty drinking water, unhygienic toilets or badly prepared food. NOT SEX.

HEPATITIS B   is transmitted sexually as well as in other ways.

It's a bit of a minefield and it's too big to sort it all out here, so forget the problems and just remember: if you think there is something wrong or you have taken part in unsafe behaviour then go and get it checked.

The GP or clinic will know and give you the right advice.

That's what they're there for.

WHERE TO GET A CONDOM

★FREE★

FAMILY PLANNING CLINICS

They do all contraception, including the morning-after pill, pregnancy testing, pregnancy counselling, smear tests. To find your nearest, look in the phone book, or ring the number in the back of this book.

★FREE★

BROOK ADVISORY CLINICS

These places are good because they are specially for young people.

They give advice and support on all sexual matters.

They give free contraceptives, free pregnancy testing, advice on abortion, the morning-after pill, advice on tests for HIV and other STDs. To find your nearest one, look in the phone book or ring the number in the back of this book.

★FREE★

GUM CLINICS
GUM stands for genito-urinary medicine.
That's everything to do with the genitals (balls, penis, vagina, anus etc) and the fluids in them (urine or pee, period blood, vaginal fluid, semen or spunk).

These places are quite often attached to a hospital, which is good because although you might have to travel further to get there it means they are completely anonymous if that's what you want. You're not likely to bump into Mrs Jones from next door or whatever.

They do everything that the BROOK (above) does but they also do tests for HIV and other STDs here.

They also offer lots of helpful advice and are willing to listen if you have a problem you can't sort out.

You can go there for all sorts of advice, not just about contraceptives. In fact you don't have to get contraceptives here, have an HIV test or a smear if you don't want to and they won't ask embarrassing questions if you're under 16.

You don't need to see your GP first.

You can make an appointment or just call in. They'll be in the phone book, or you can ring the number in the back of this book.

★FREE★ HIV/AIDS ADVICE SUPPORT CENTRES

Most of these have free condoms around the place. Just go and pick some up. Also a good place to get leaflets. We list some of these centres in the back of this book. Ring National AIDS helpline (0800 567 123) for your local one.

★£££££★

SUPERMARKETS
VIRGIN RECORD STORES
THE BODY SHOP
CHEMISTS

Here they cost. Condoms, that is; you can't get other contraceptives over the counter due to the fact that they either need to be fitted or prescribed.

Condoms cost around £1 for three.

You can get spermicides and water based lubricants here as well, (if you use oily or greasy ones, like Vaseline, it will damage the condom).

The FEMIDOM costs around £3.95 for three (that's the new female condom). They CAN be used with oil-based lubricants.

PUBS
YOUTH CLUBS

In quite a lot of places these days there are condom machines in the gents' and ladies' loos. More in the gents still, I have to say, but the ladies are catching up.

Condoms come in packets of three and you'll need a £1 coin. PS Graffiti on a condom machine said:

'This is the worst chewing gum I've ever tasted!' (geddit?)

I reckon the place where you're most likely to find out everything you want is the BROOK.

Every centre has a specialist service for young people. Quite a lot of FAMILY PLANNING CLINICS do as well but it depends a lot on where you live.

A lot of doctors have a family planning service attached to their practice as well, and you should give them a call first to check out when they're open.

Remember, you don't have to do anything you don't want to and you can give any name you want (though it's helpful to pick one you can remember).

■■■■■■■■■■■■■■■■■■■■■■■■■■■■■■■

ALBERT SQUARE There's a condom machine in THE QUEEN VIC. So far EASTENDERS has talked about safer sex in 30 different episodes.

■■■■■■■■■■■■■■■■■■■■■■■■■■■■■■■

HOW TO PUT ON A CONDOM

Putting on a condom is easy. Either you or your partner can do it.

If you feel nervous about it, try practising on a banana or a cucumber, or even your two fingers, sticking up and held together. Improvise!

This is how you do it:

1. Make sure the foreskin is pulled back (if you've got one).
2. Squeeze the tip of the condom between your thumb and first finger to get rid of any trapped air.

3. Hold the rolled up condom at the tip of the erect penis (the penis has to be hard).
4. Unroll it over the penis to the base. (If it doesn't unroll easily, it might be inside out – take it off and look).

5. Leave a little space at the top to allow for stretching. (In other words don't force it all the way down – there's enough of it to cover the whole penis easily)

6. If you or your partner are a bit dry and want to use some cream to make penetration easier, make sure you use a water-based cream like KY jelly or special lubricant (sold in chemists next to the condoms). Put it around the entrance to the vagina, or on the condom.

7. After sex, withdraw the penis while it's still hard, holding on to the open end of the condom (that's at the base of the penis) to stop it slipping off.

8. Wrap it in a tissue and throw it away.

9. Only use a condom once. Then throw it away. If you want to have sex again, use another one.

★ RED ALERT ★ ★ RED ALERT ★

Creams like VASELINE or FACE cream or COLD CREAM (baby lotion, oil, suntan oils) contain grease which can rot the rubber the condom is made from in minutes, and if that happened you wouldn't be safe any more! (You won't be able to see it, but if you looked under a microscope there would be lots of little holes)

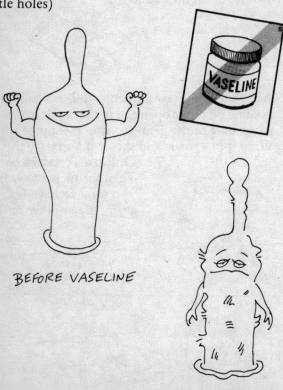

BEFORE VASELINE

AFTER VASELINE

When buying condoms, make sure you get one with the British safety standard, the Kitemark, printed on the packet.

Only wear one condom at a time. Two will not make sex any safer. In fact it's the opposite: if you wear two together they are more likely to slip off.

FACT: there are loads of different condoms around. Check out what suits you best.
Huw from the National AIDS Trust says:
'Finding out that there were lots of different condoms changed my life. Shop around until you find one you like – there's all different colours, thicknesses and smells. Try all sorts until you feel comfortable.'

You can get stronger ones for anal sex – look for the words extra strong or extra safe on the packet.

Other words for condoms: Johnny, Rubber, French Letter, Trojan, Jiffy, Willy warmer, Welly . . .

QUESTIONS AND ANSWERS ABOUT CONDOMS

I know I should use a condom but I'm embarrassed to ask my boyfriend to use one – he says he hates them.
He'd hate having AIDS a lot more. This thing is bigger than a little bit of embarrassment – it could be life or death. Here's ten reasons you could give for using a condom:

✤ *I care about me and you. And that means not being at risk from STDs.*

✤ *I don't want us to be worried about pregnancy.*

✤ *I want to show you that they can be fun if we put one on together.*

✤ *(for boys) I want to be inside you as long as possible and wearing one can make me last longer.*

✤ *I never have sex unless it's safer sex.*

- ✹ *All my mates use them, I'd feel stupid if we didn't.*

- ✹ *I want us to be really safe so another contraceptive on its own won't do.*

- ✹ *I'm nervous about using them, and want you to show me.*

- ✹ *I know you'd think I'm stupid if we don't.*

■■■■■■■■■■■■■■■■■■■■■■■■■■■■

The average condom stretches to about 1.5 metres long and can hold up to 2 litres of water. So they'll fit you, however big you are! (If it looks too small it might be because it's inside out and won't unroll.)

AN AVERAGE CONDOM CAN HOLD UP TO 2 LITRES OF WATER

■■■■■■■■■■■■■■■■■■■■■■■■■■■

I'm Roman Catholic and my Church forbids the use of contraception including condoms. I don't know what to do.

I asked Martin, from Positively Irish Action on AIDS (phone number in the back of this book) about this one. Martin lives in Hackney, has two frogs and lots of tadpoles in his backyard. He loves gardening and going to pubs.

There's discussion in the Church about all this and there's some confusion around condoms for safer sex and condoms for contraception.

The traditional view is that it's OK to use condoms for the 'prevention of disease and infection', but not as an artificial means of preventing pregnancy (the rhythm method is acceptable according to the Church and so is abstention ie not having sex).

But the Church also says you can't go against your conscience, and what that means is up to you. If you decide your conscience demands you use condoms, then you're not necessarily going against the Church by doing so.

We live in County Cork, and can't get condoms over here.

Martin . . .

Well, condoms are freely available in Northern Ireland and you'll find a lot of people get them over there.

There's also mail order firms where you can get them through the post.

Condoms are available on prescription from a doctor, although it's true that finding a sympathetic one might be a problem.

Ring one of the organisations listed in the back for how to get in touch with sympathetic doctors.

I live in a small town, and can't get to the local clinic. The doctor knows my family really well. So I don't want to go to him.

Martin. . . .

There are some good organisations you can ring to get advice, some in England, some in Northern Ireland and one in the Republic.

All the people there have knowledge on all kinds of issues: contraception, HIV, gay issues, help and advice.

They will also know sympathetic doctors and Church ministers in your area.

Give them a ring and have a chat. Numbers are in the back of the book.

(This is also true for the Asian and Jewish communities: look in back of book, there's an organisation for everyone. Sue)

■■■■■■■■■■■■■■■■■■■■■■■■■■■■

Today's condom is thin, thin, thin, just 0.03mm thick. Less than half the thickness of a single strand of human hair.
Feel that!

CHEER UP, ROBIN. YOUR HAIR IS TWICE AS THICK AS THIS CONDOM

■■■■■■■■■■■■■■■■■■■■■■■■■■■■

People say that condoms don't always stop you getting pregnant. Is it the same with HIV?
It's certainly true that some people have got pregnant while using condoms.

There could be several reasons for this:

1. *The condom may not have been put on properly or it may have slipped off during intercourse.*
2. *It may have deteriorated because some kind of oil-based cream/liquid has been used.*
3. *Sexual fluid (containing sperm) may have entered the woman's vagina before the condom was put on.*

If any of these things happen during sex then there is a possibility of pregnancy.

And also a possibility of HIV transmission. So I

guess the thing to say is that it's important to use condoms properly with a spermicide like NN9 (Nonoxyl 9) for added safety.

If you want to you could also use vaginal pessaries (waxy tablets put into the vagina) containing NN9 for added safety.

NN9 is a liquid that contains chemicals which kill sperm and HIV.

Many condoms have this on them already as do water-based lubricants.

Some women choose to take the Pill for contraception AND use a condom for protection from HIV and STDs – a neat little double package that makes them safe in every way.

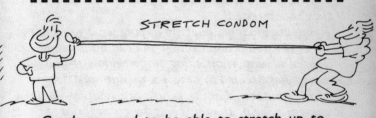

STRETCH CONDOM

Condoms need to be able to stretch up to 650% in order to pass the BRITISH SAFETY STANDARDS (KITEMARK)
Do you know how big that is????

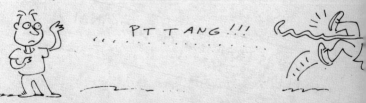

Should I tell my younger brother about HIV and condoms?

Depends how old he is.

It's never a bad idea to talk to people about safer sex if they're interested.

Remember to talk about not having sex if you don't want it and about other things you can do instead.

The most important thing to get across is that if someone has decided to have sex then it must always be with condoms. Giving people information about sex doesn't mean they're going to go out and start doing it. What's important is knowing the facts, so you can make the right choices when the time comes.

ADVICE IS FREE from the NATIONAL AIDS HELPLINE 0800 567 123

Chapter 3
GILL'S STORY

OCT 30th

Went to Lisa's party on Saturday.

They played some good music, WORLDS APART and MADONNA. Then Gary went and put on Elvis Costello!

Course the whole room groaned, but in the end it was quite a laugh.

They did some real smoochy numbers and everyone had to change partners till the end of the record.

I got a bit cheesed off actually, Mark started slow dancing with Jan – and I reckon they started touching each other up, well not exactly, but you know what I mean, the wrong kind of close, her nuzzling him in the neck, stuff like that.

He says it's 'cos he was a bit drunk.

Well, that's no excuse! God, what am I supposed to do? Laugh it off and say, 'That's all right, darling, get off with whoever you like, I'll still be waiting, like the good little wifey I'm not, thank you very much!'

It all got a big sick after that, there was a gang, I didn't know them, taking drugs in the kitchen. I think they thought nobody noticed, but of course everybody did, and they were out of it, way off their heads. I felt a bit scared actually.

Anyway, we stomped off home and now we're not speaking.

I don't see why I should. It's up to him to apologise. But I do feel rotten.

Nov 20th

I've got an appointment at the clinic tomorrow. Only for tests, not going in or anything.

The results came back 'inconclusive' so the doctor suggested I go the hospital 'just to clear it up once and for all, we don't want to go on having these problems down there do we?' Notice, there's that 'we' again.

But he did say it wouldn't be anything serious, 'catch it in the early stages and there's rarely a problem'.

I'm scared of cancer, so many people in my family have gone with it, makes me think it's in the blood.

Nov 21

Lot of blah really.

I don't know what I'm fussing for. Mark's right of course. I get into a flap and then it's all over nothing.

It was really quick. You walk in, see the guy on the desk and wait to be called.

Then this lady turned up, took me to her office and told me all the ins and outs of the various tests.

Said the HIV test was special. Asked me what I knew and who I'd talk to about it.

Then she said I didn't have to decide right there and then, I could wait and think about it then come back on another day, but I just said yes to all of them, might as well clear it up now, otherwise you only have to keep coming back all the time.

The nurse took my urine sample, 'first thing in the morning, mid-stream flow' . . . which means you wee a bit first and then go in the bottle, (I have to say my aim is getting better); checked my blood pressure, another scrape, blood test and then all my reflexes (that's the kneejerk bit), then down the next floor to a female doctor who looked inside this time and felt around.

Said it all seemed perfectly normal.

All I have to do now is go back in a week for the results.

It's turned out quite good actually, because the pills have practically cleared the cystitis now and I've four days left to finish the bathroom.

Nov 23

Well, I have to say it looks fab, I've done most of it – the walls and the ceiling.

Got to stick with the old stuff on the windows and the door for the time being. A tin of gloss would be another £10.90 and we can't really stretch to that.

You wouldn't really notice though 'cos it's all so bright and fresh.

Nov 24

Lisa's been over. Helped me finish it off.

Darren's chucked her in again.

She's mad, that girl, I don't know why she's so upset, after all the things he's done.

But she loves him, well, she thinks she does.

'Course she's devastated. I didn't dare tell her that we'd seen him out with Natalie, down the rink, and that was two weeks back! She's well shot of him.

I suppose she's right though, there isn't much choice up here, not like London or something and where's she going to meet another bloke?

Tried to get her to go for Nigel, he's been smooching after her for months now but she won't look at him. No, she loves Darren, he's all she can think of, and what if he saw her with another bloke? She'd never get him back. All that rubbish.

Well, I didn't like to say but there's no chance of that anyway, he was only going out with her because of her sister in the first place!

And now she's off to college he wouldn't be seen dead with her. It sounds awful but I know it's true, because he told Mark.

Said he did get off with her sister as well, at the same time as he was going out with Lisa, but I don't believe that, not for a minute.

Anyway, we had a great time taking it all out on the bathroom walls, painting 'DARREN's a B....' and stuff before we covered it up.

WHO'S AT RISK AND WHO'S NOT?

The big question in all this is who's in line to contract HIV and who isn't.

Some would say everyone.

But that's not quite true. . . .

The SUN newspaper said: 'STRAIGHT SEX CANNOT GIVE YOU AIDS – OFFICIAL' and then went on to say . . . 'the killer disease AIDS can only be caught by homosexuals, bisexuals, junkies or anyone who has received a tainted blood transfusion. . . .'

A week later they had to publish an article saying 'The Sun was wrong to state that it is impossible to catch AIDS from heterosexual sex. We apologise.'

The whole business of HIV is confusing, and some of the less responsible newspapers have published a lot of rubbish about it. People pick up untrue 'facts' from this, and will pass them on to you as gospel.

Some people would believe newspapers if they said the world was a floating tea tray, and we were all sitting in a cup of tea in the middle of it! But for real, researched, carefully accurate facts, stick to what the experts say and don't depend on scaremongers or 'grapevine' talk for your facts.

DIGESTIVE BISCUIT REQUESTING PERMISSION TO LAND, CAPTAIN

OK, SO WHO CAN'T GET HIV?

Well, anyone who's a virgin who's never had any sexual experience, including intercourse either anally or vaginally, and who knows for sure that they never will in the future and will never expose themselves to any other form of high-risk behaviour, ever, for the rest of their lives.

Does this sound unlikely?

Does this sound like you?

Or Mum or Dad?!

Or the lady next door?

Well, maybe, but if you're a more ordinary person like me, you are at risk if you take part in sexual behaviour or drug abuse and don't stay safe.

Because you can't tell who's carrying the virus and who's not!

What's more, the person carrying the virus may not know either!

And it goes on. . . . The person you're sleeping with may have slept with someone who slept with someone who slept with someone who is HIV+.

If that first person transmits the virus it could go all down the line until it gets to you!

So when you have sex with someone you're having sex with all their previous partners as well.

And they are with yours.

It doesn't matter if YOU'VE only slept with ONE other person, and so has your partner – or if you're a virgin and your partner's only had sex with ONE other person, because you're going to be having sex with every person THAT person slept with and so on back down the line. So even if you've had very little sexual experience you're just as much IN DANGER.

Whichever way you look at it, it's an awful lot of people and any one of them could be HIV+.

Penetrative sex without a condom is bad news every time.

Carry one just in case. There's always going to be someone who's taking risks, so if you're not using your condom, pass it on to them.

Condoms are for life. What's HIV for?

HIV – A FAMILY TREE

JACKIE

is HIV + She caught the virus because she used to inject drugs and once shared a needle. For a while, she went out with

JOHN

But he didn't like the drug side of her and split up. Although he doesn't know it, he is now HIV + On holiday he sleeps with

MANDY

without a condom. She becomes HIV + (but doesn't know it). A year later, she sleeps with

GIORGIOU

who has had other partners. He becomes HIV + (but doesn't know it). He sleeps with

CHRISTINA

(who makes him use a condom) She does not catch the virus.

BETHAN

(who makes him withdraw) She becomes HIV + (but doesn't know it) She gets engaged to

CRAIG

who is a virgin. They sleep together. He becomes HIV + (but doesn't know it) when they split up, he has two other girlfriends

CHANTAL

who is a virgin. Because Craig has only slept with one other person, she thinks they're safe. She becomes HIV+.

LUCY

who has had other partners. She uses a condom and does not catch the virus.

HIV AROUND THE WORLD

There's two things here to say about HIV and travelling.

The first point is that people are travelling around the world all the time, so thinking you're going to be OK because you live in a country where the numbers of HIV+ cases are low is wrong.

The WHO (World Health Organisation) reckons that around 5,000 people across the world are becoming HIV+ every day, and that's only the beginning.

Numbers are going up all the time.

Lots of people have contracted HIV from holiday romances or sex with someone from another country.

Holiday romances? – WEAR A CONDOM

QUESTION AND ANSWERS ABOUT HIV

Can you tell from your symptoms if you are HIV +?
You can't! You might be completely healthy but still be carrying the virus. Some people stay healthy for ten years being HIV+. The only way you can tell, to be sure, is to have a test.

What about drugs? Is it all or just some?
It's not the drugs themselves that contain the virus.

It's what you do with them that can be dangerous.

Sharing needles and injecting drugs is a very easy way to pass on HIV, because infected blood remaining behind in the barrel of the syringe can easily be injected by another user into his or her body along with the drug.

Smoking, sniffing and swallowing drugs contain no risk of transmitting infected blood, although they put you at risk of a whole host of other things, like death from overdose.

And in a way they can give you HIV, because if you're really stoned or drunk it's easier to get carried away and forget about using a condom.

Drugs include things like booze and cigarettes as well as illegal stuff like Ecstasy, dope, speed or heroin (smack).

CHRISTINE CHESTER from THE HUNGER-
FORD DRUGS PROJECT says:
*'It's hard to assert yourself with any kind of rational
decision when you are completely off your face,
regardless of what you are off your face with!*

*. . . many a time someone thinks they've been
infected by sharing, when in fact they've got it
through unsafe sex as a RESULT of sharing! (Sharing
means using the same needles or syringes.)'*

STAR INTERVIEW

John is HIV+. He's a dad, works as an architect, lives in Strathclyde.

He and his wife get an Indian takeaway every Friday night and he always has the same: chicken Kurma, pilau rice and two poppadums.

'I suppose having two children growing up, I feel very strongly about young people growing up with the risks of HIV. I feel it's extremely difficult to get the message across. Maybe that's not right, maybe it's not difficult to get the message across, it's just difficult for people to take it on board.

To actually do something about it, to think, "This means me, I'm responsible for my own life and my own health." It's really frustrating to know that I'm positive and yet to be unsure about whether my own children practise safer sex.

I've got it, but if I can go out and prevent even one person from getting it then that will be OK.

I don't know if it can be like that, I don't know if things are ever that simple.'

Chapter 4
GILL'S STORY

Dec 12

I went back.

I've got AIDS.

Dec 20th

Is it really only a week ago? Somehow I can't quite believe that.

I feel as though I walked into that hospital Gill Robinson, typist, 5 foot 6 inches tall, mousey brown hair, medium build, and walked out one of the untouchables.

I went down the street, over the traffic lights (they were green and some bloke sat on the horn, leaned out of the car window and shouted something rude), and into Mcdonalds. I ordered a Big Mac, double strawberry milkshake, 2 portions of French fries and a summer fruit pie. And a coke.

After all, if you've just had your sentence what's the point in doing Weightwatchers?

I hardly ate a thing.

Well, that's what it is, isn't it? A sentence.

Dec 22nd

I can't describe it.

I keep trying; going out, trying to do the Christmas shopping and coming back with things that nobody is going to want.

A plastic bath duck for Gran, a book for Auntie Joan.

It had a lovely cover on the front. When I got it home I found out it was about pony trekking in the Hebrides.

Auntie Joan's at least 14 stone. The poor thing wouldn't have a chance.

I went to Underwoods, I must have been standing at the sock counter so long they thought I was going to nick something.

This big bloke comes up to me, 'Excuse me, miss, may I look in your bag please, just security miss, the IRA, bombs and that.'

I must have jumped a mile, I thought somehow he knew and he was going to take me off to the police station for being HIV positive.

I feel really scared: that they're going to find out at work, that the hospital is going to tell my boss and my family.

That the word AIDS is going to be daubed in red paint all over my front door.

It feels like it's written across my forehead.

God, my family! My mum's going to go off the wall. I can't tell her, how can I?

She'll never see me again.

Two days to Christmas. I have to go down to Shipley tomorrow.

I can't believe this.

I'm sorry but it's ridiculous. What did I ever do to the world that they went and gave me AIDS?

Dec 23rd

I got a bit of sleep last night and I'm beginning to think a little more clearly. The obvious answer is to go back to the hospital and get them to do some more tests.

I mean, doctors don't always know what they're doing.

We think they're so high and mighty but they aren't always.

God, only last month there was that story in the Daily News about those two caesarean babies that got mixed up; went to the wrong mums, and one of them was Chinese!

I mean, for god's sake, if they can do that, I mean, well, they can get a test result wrong.

The tests I took weren't the same anyway.

At the doctor's I had a scrape thing with this wooden thing and my blood pressure and urine and it wasn't until the hospital that they took the blood.

Well, how many lots of blood do they have to take in one day?

I didn't see her put a label on it or anything.

I'm going back there, straight after Christmas, and if they're wrong I'm going to tell everybody, the world. And the newspapers. They've got no right to treat people like that.

Dec 27th

It's taking me a long time to adjust to all this.

As you see I've come back here pretty quick.

Christmas was the worst I think I've ever spent.

I had no desire to go back home at all.

My little sister was prattling on. I never realised quite how self-centred kids are at seven.

Why didn't she have the Mario 2 for her gameboy? Where was the Barbie Doll Auntie Trudy promised? . . . She's still missing two things from her Little Pony set etc. etc.

On and on it went.

My dad as usual slumped in front of the telly stuffing out with mince pies, and smoking those cigarillos things. Because it's Christmas and he wants to look sophisticated when the neighbours come round.

And of course, all my mates from home.

Sarah has had a baby.

The sweetest little thing . . . only six weeks old and so tiny.

You should have seen his tiny hands and his fingers all curled round.

I was scared to touch him in case I infected him. I

didn't know what to do, 'Go on, go on' she kept saying, 'pick him up, he won't break.'

And the stupid thing was that if she'd known about me she'd have run a mile. I wouldn't have been allowed near him.

So I did hold him, just for a little, and I couldn't hold back the tears.

He was so small, so trusting, nestling up to me, with that sweet milky smell that only little babies have.

This will never be a part of my life. I can hardly bear to feel these thoughts.

That little baby. He was so small.

She complained a lot. Says he cries all night, keeps her up, the guy's cleared off and it's all down to her.

How lucky she is.

Dec 29th

Went back to the hospital today.

The woman was really nice.

Louise, she said she was called.

Sat me down and gave me a cup of tea. With sugar in it.

I don't take sugar.

Why do they always do that when things are bad?

You always get a cup of tea.

I wonder what they do in India. 'Oh, you're feeling upset, have an onion bhajee.'

Weird what you think of at times like this.

She kept talking to me, softly and low, with pauses, kept asking me if I understood, how I felt and all. I kept thinking what she would look like in a sari.

She had wavy hair, sort of down to her shoulders, not very well cut.

You'd think in a job like that she could afford to go to the hairdressers a bit more often.

I almost asked her how much she got paid to 'counsel' people like me.

Thought I'd recommend Raymond's off the High Street.

What I did get was that they will run more tests, but there's no way that the ones they've already done could be wrong.

And that my reaction is quite normal and things will get better.

She said something about my previous partners and getting hold of them in case they've got it too.

Said they'd do it for me if I wanted or we could talk some more later.

Previous partners?

I don't know ... what about Mark?

She gave me some leaflets to read and said I wasn't going to die just yet.

No, she didn't say that, I don't know what she said, but I am well at the moment so although it's serious I won't notice the difference in my body.

What? I don't know. I can't get my head round this at all.

FACTS ABOUT THE HIV TEST

If you want to have an HIV test there are several ways of getting one.

It's probably not too hot an idea to go to your doctor's, because it goes down in your records.

If you are sixteen, they are confidential and your parents won't be allowed to see them, but doctors aren't HIV specialists and might see fit to give you a lecture along the way.

I went to a doctor when I was touring in Cambridge when I was about eighteen, because I'd got an infection that turned out to be NSU (non specific urethritis – a sexually transmitted disease).

The doctor was an old guy who took it on himself to give me this great lecture about sex and sexuality, how promiscuous I was being and how it's best to be a virgin when you marry!

Well, please!

Surely what it's all about is knowing the facts and making your own decisions about them?

Of course, he was a bit potty and most doctors aren't like that at all, but the people at the GUM clinics, BROOK clinics and FPA's are a bit more streetwise and won't give you the third degree.

Is it a good idea to take the HIV test?

There are all kinds of questions to think about before going to take a test.

And there's always a counsellor at the clinic to talk it through with, which is great.

There's absolutely no pressure at all to have the test and you can change your mind any time you like.

I guess what's important to say is that if you feel you've taken risks and may have been exposed to the virus, then maybe you should think about it.

Anything you're concerned about can be checked out, and the BROOK, FAMILY PLANNING or GUM CLINIC is the place to do that.

The people there get paid to answer questions and sort out concerns, not just to run tests, so don't feel you're putting on them – you're actually keeping them in work!

STAR INTERVIEW

Dennis Gray is a health adviser at the Kobler Centre (a specialist HIV centre). Dennis is from Melbourne, Australia but is now living over here. He jogs every morning in Regent's Park, cycles to work and used to be a graphic designer.

'*After booking in at reception, anyone having the HIV test would come and see the health adviser (that's me) first. The reason for that is the chance to talk things over, to see whether or not it's a good idea to have one at the moment.*

One of the important things we have to check is that if someone has done something risky in the last three months, then the test may not show that. That's quite important! The test will show through all the time BEFORE that period.

I would normally start by saying:

"What's brought you in to have a test?"

. . . I think often people come to have a test at times of change in their lives, or they are not very sure whether they have caught something – if they have had sex without a condom, for example.

Most people go through with the test, some don't. We NEVER put pressure on people to have the test.

As to the test itself, well, there can be quite a lot of waiting around. You go to reception, come to see the Health Adviser, and then anyone coming in for the test will have to see the doctor.

The doctor would sign various forms as would the person having the test.

You sign clearly in the notes your permission to have your blood tested for HIV. The doctor will then offer other tests if required, such as those for sexually transmitted diseases, for example. After that the person will go to see the nurse who will take the blood, and then you're off!

There is a rapid test where you can get the result the next day. When the person comes back, the Health Adviser would give the result.

Normally the result is given by the doctor or nurse. With people I would see for pre-test counselling, and perhaps with a high risk of testing positive, I might ask them if they would like me to give them the result. It's a lot more personal this way.

As you can imagine, when someone has been given a positive result, they are usually in a state of shock.

Perhaps they are not taking in too much at all.

We'll also suggest follow-up appointments, which most people will want to do.

I'll suggest two or three days' time. At that session I'll probably spend about 50 minutes with them, and I'll just see what they need, what they want.

I think a lot of people, when they get a diagnosis, feel they are not worthy of attention and care. I try to show them that's not right.'

THE TEST

Caroline took the test – here's her description of what happened:

'1. I walked in the GUM clinic without an appointment and was asked to fill in this form.
 2. I had to wait. Then I saw the Health Adviser.
 3. A nurse came up and said Hi.
 4. She asked me to take off my jacket and my jumper and roll up my sleeve.
 5. They put one of those grey blood pressure sleeves on and blew it up.
 6. They rubbed some cold antiseptic on my arm.
 7. She said it wouldn't hurt a bit. She suggested I look at the wall.
 8. It did! But not a lot, a bit like an injection, or a sharp pinprick.
 9. She asked if I was frightened of needles because I looked so scared! It was really quick. She said everyone felt like that.
10. I asked her if she was scared handling all this blood that might be infected and needles and that.
11. She said it wasn't a worry as long as they took proper precautions.
12. She showed me a cut on her hand which she'd put a plaster over. Wounds are only risky if they're open and sore. If any blood gets spilled they mop it up with a mixture of one part bleach to 9 parts water.

     If there are any viruses in the blood they are killed immediately by this.
13. She was wearing thin plastic disposable gloves.
     She threw the used needle into a "sharps" bin.

It's just like a plastic bin but everything in it gets burnt later. Instead of going out with the rubbish.

14. Well, it wasn't too bad, she put a plaster on my arm. I had to keep it on for an hour and that's it.

15. There were loads of free condoms and leaflets at the clinic. She said take as many as you like, so I got a selection, some minty green ones, some ribbed ones and some hypo-allergenic, not all for me I reckoned I'd pass 'em round.

16. Anyone looking in my bag would reckon I'm well sussed!

17. The counsellor said I should come back in two weeks for the result and we made an appointment there and then.

18. I went back and she told me my result was negative.'

Here's some comments from a few people who have taken the test and what they felt:

DEANNE:
'*I was diagnosed very early on in infection.*

I'd been on holiday in Spain and I hadn't used condoms. I came back and three weeks later I was very ill. I was taken to hospital and I had Hepatitis A and a cyst on my ovary.

Because of the cyst I had to see a gynaecologist.

I got better and went back to college.

A few months later I went back to see the same person and he examined me and took blood and that was it.

I went back to college and around four months later I was dragged out of lectures by my head of department.

She said you've got to go and see your doctor

straight away. I went to him and he rushed me upstairs, he said "Well, there's no other way of telling you this, you've got AIDS," and I just sat there.

Then he said "Don't get pregnant, if you're in a car crash try not to spill your blood on anyone else".

And that was it. He gave me a lift home, and I went home and drank a bottle of brandy.'

Ian had the one-day test:
'I had the pre-test counselling and then went and gave a blood sample. This was 10am and I was told to come back at 4pm for the result.

I'm on the dole, but if I had been working then I doubt that I would have been able to on that day.

I just wandered around window-shopping, counting the minutes until I had to go back.

I went back in the afternoon and waited for my turn to be called in.

Everything was a blur and I could not concentrate on anything for more than a few minutes at a time.

I was convinced that I was positive and started to suffer from depression . . .

Going back in for the result I was relieved to find out that I was negative . . .'

WHERE CAN YOU HAVE A TEST?

For a list of the GUM clinics or STD CLINICs look in the telephone book under VENEREAL DISEASES.

Also the NATIONAL AIDS HELPLINE (number at the back of this book) gives you info on where to get tested locally.

● ●

FACT: Across the world 13 million people are reckoned to be HIV+ (*Source: World Health Organisation*)

● ●

STAND UP AND BE COUNTED

I, Susanna Dawson, have never had a test for HIV.

I have had unsafe sex in the past; that is, I've had sex without using a condom. I've not slept with anyone that I have known to have been involved in high-risk behaviour but as we have said over and over in this book, we don't know everything about our partners or who they have slept with. Right now I'm too scared to take the test. It may be that if I get involved in a permanent relationship I will go and do that.

What I do know is that HIV and AIDS has changed the way I think about things.

I don't sleep with people any more unless I feel there's a real chance of a relationship, and if I do, it's always with a condom.

QUESTIONS AND ANSWERS ABOUT THE HIV TEST

When should you have a HIV test? How often?
You've got to be clear of any high-risk behaviour for a full three months before you take the HIV test, because it can take that long for the antibodies to show up in your body. So if you have had a test and then have unsafe sex or share needles, you should have another one.

It's not really a one-off thing.

On the other hand, there's no point in going to have a test unless you're worried about what you've been doing.

How can I be sure nobody will know I've had a test?
Dr NICOLA SMITH M.R.C. research fellow from the KOBLER CENTRE says:

'We haven't had a problem here with information getting into the hands of the wrong people. Absolutely everything is completely confidential.'

If you're really unsure about it, remember, they don't have to know your name. There's a clinic in London which has tested more than 130 Margaret Thatchers, and most of them are guys!

Most of the clinics these days just give you a number.

Can you have sex with someone who is HIV+?
Sue: It's a difficult question this one and I'm not the right person to answer it, so here's what MALCOLM, who's HIV+, thinks.

Malcolm: 'The answer to that is yes, you can. The full list of safer sexual practices is now easily available.

I think you need to be very clear about what "safer sex" is, so you can choose the kind of sex that is right for you.

Both partners need to be caring about it, both for themselves and each other.

I do still have a sex life, but it's different now and I approach it in a different way.

I'm more cautious and less relaxed, and I think it will take time to gain my confidence again, but I also think this is to be expected so I don't beat myself up about it!'

How do you know if someone is HIV+?
That's the best question of the lot because YOU DON'T unless they tell you. And anyway, they might not know.

So look after number one, accept that you don't know and take care of yourself.

Would they lie?
Have you ever lied about anything to anyone? Ever?
So have I and that's your answer.

Are you safe if you know everyone you've slept with?
No, because you don't know who's positive and who's not.

And you don't know about your lover either. It's either no sex or sex with a condom.

Are you safe if your partner tells you they're negative?
Tricky one this.

You aren't going to know whether they're telling the truth or not, and anyway, seeing as we can't tell who's HIV+ and who's HIV−, they might not know themselves.

Best to accept that you don't know and therefore use a condom every time you have sex.

Should I or my partner get tested?
Depends.

If you want to stop using condoms, it's maybe a good idea to check you're both HIV negative first.

Then you have to be sure (if you're both negative) that you will be completely faithful to each other.

Think about your feelings if you're positive too. Good idea to talk to a counsellor about it.

Try the Brook or a GUM clinic.

What if someone finds out I've rung an AIDS helpline?

*They won't. If you ring the National AIDS helpline, the people on the other end of the line are trained not to ask you anything you don't want to answer. They won't ask your name, number or address and will only help you. The number doesn't come up on the phone bill so nobody needs to know you've rung, and they answer 24 hours a day, 365 days a year so you can ring at a time when everyone in your house is out. Nothing is too **unimportant** to ring them about. They can help with everything around the subject, even silly little worries, and will sort out all you need to know.*

If English isn't your first language, you can ring someone up and speak in your own language. Look in the back of this book for the numbers.

Chapter 5
GILL'S STORY

March 15th

It's taking me a long time to adjust to all this.

I've had a really tough time just recently.

I do know now that being HIV+ is not an automatic death sentence.

Michael (my doctor) says treatments are improving all the time and we're talking years not months.

I do know this, in my head; it's just hard to believe it.

Every time I go to the loo, when I have a period, I look down and think, it's there, this virus that is in there, hidden, running around infecting people.

It's so difficult because I feel fine. There's been nothing wrong with me at all, swollen glands once or twice but that's nothing, everyone gets that.

It's like I don't have to believe because nothing's happening, sometimes I wish I might get a bit sick so I could come to terms with all this.

Stupid thought, I know.

And yet, all the time it has to be this hidden secret, knowing that if I told my friends, they'd have it all over town in a minute.

I'd lose my job, I'd lose my friends, people would

look at me in the street, all that kind of thing and more if it got out.

As it is, it seems a wise precaution to change doctors.

They make jokes about AIDS at work and I laugh, like everyone else.

Isn't it enough having this virus without all this?

Name me another illness where instead of support and kindness you get kicked in the face? You can't, can you?

Where you're made to feel like some outcast, or animal or Martian or something.

Oh, and by the way, Mark's got it too.

March 25th

It had got to the stage where the excuses were running out. I seemed to be washing my hair once too often, not feeling up to it, too tired, that sort of thing. And he couldn't understand why I was insisting on condoms when we did do it . . . all that kind of stuff.

In the end the rows got so bad that I thought we might as well be arguing about what was really going on instead of these pathetic excuses all the time.

He didn't believe them anyway, knows me far too well for that.

It was when he thought I had another guy that I began to worry.

But where do you begin? How do you start to tell your fella about something as big as this?

Especially when that fella happens to be the only one you've ever felt you really loved? The only one you've even begun to consider spending the rest of your life with.

The one you've dreamed of sharing a little house in the country with, one cat, one pig, one rabbit, roses round the door and all that.

And yes, the big one, kiddies too.

I tried to tell him for a whole week.

I kept waiting for the right moment.

Before tea, after tea . . . first thing in the morning, last thing at night.

I kept waiting for times when we'd be alone; and then never quite getting there.

He kept going on at me: why was I such a moody cow? What was the matter? Was it something at work?

Then he said it must be PMT.

If only it was.

March 26th

I did tell him in the end. It was really pathetic, I offered to clean his biking boots.

He was dead chuffed, put his feet up in front of the telly and watched the Superbowl.

I waited for halftime; of course it never came.

I got right down to the last bit of boot; I even started doing the buckles on the straps with metal polish, and then I just kind of muttered it.

Told him I'd been to the hospital, that the results of the test had come back, that they tested again and that I had this virus.

I'm exhausted just writing this down.

He didn't hear of course, was concentrating on the Superbowl, asked me to wait until it finished.

No, I said. He had to know now.

Well, I said again that I had this virus and he slid off the sofa, put his arm round me and said well, it's OK, it was good to find out what was wrong and they'd give me tablets.

He was being all nice 'cos I'd done his boots.

Then I told him it wasn't OK because the virus was HIV.

He didn't get it at all.

And then he did.

I expected him to hit the roof, to rant and rave.

He didn't. He went completely silent.

I think that was worse.

March 29th

I guess talking it through with Mark, or rather not talking, because he seems to refuse to accept the truth about either of us, has kind of made me think about the family.

I have to tell them too.

That'll be a nice birthday present.

April 15th

My birthday has come and gone. Hardly felt worth celebrating. 'Cept mum suggested I go down to Shipley for the weekend and I told her.

You know what she said?

'Well, at least you had the decency not to spoil Christmas'.

Nothing about me and how I feel.

It was all the shame of it; how could she have raised such a dirty daughter, what kind of example is that for Tracy, how's she going to face everyone at work?

I just sat there and took it all. I couldn't argue back.

And then she started washing the kitchen floor, getting out the rubber gloves, the bleach bottle, and scrubbed like it was going out of fashion.

She washed down all the formica, all the shelves, 'How could you let me down like this, people don't get AIDS in Shipley.'

I made myself a cup of tea. She threw the cup away. I found it later in the bin.

I left. I don't know what to say, really.

June 2nd

I would have thought, wouldn't you, that if we're both positive we could do it without any fear of passing on the virus — seeing as we've both already got it?

But now they reckon that we should use condoms too, and we've been putting ourselves at risk all this time.

Apparently there are different strains of this bloody thing and we can re-infect each other.

Which would weaken the body even more.

Thanks, bug.

July 22nd

Things are not good. Everything seems tainted by being HIV positive.

We're 'polite' to each other more often than not these days.

That or endless rows.

All the fun and spark seems to have gone; nothing feels easy, it's as though I'm walking on glass all the time, treading on eggshells, not knowing when he's going to explode.

It's like I have to think really carefully before I say anything, he always seems to take it the wrong way, or he accuses me of getting at him.

Everything I do seems to be wrong these days.

Aug 1st

I thought it might be nice if we went away for a couple of days.

Nothing posh, just Blackpool or somewhere, get a B & B and have a laugh for a change.

You know what he said? 'Don't be so bloody stupid. Who would let us sleep in their sheets? They'd have to burn them afterwards!'

Aug 3rd

I can't see how this is helping, him being so angry all the time.

OK, I know I'm angry too, but why can't we talk about it?

He's spent hours and hours making me write out lists of the names of guys I've been with (not that there's been very many) and who they've slept with, and who he's slept with and . . . and their partner's partners and the partners of them; and on and on it goes.

He doesn't believe that the clinic traced them, that they've all tested negative, that we've talked about it.

I bring him back leaflets from the clinic. He throws them in the bin.

You want to know where he gets his so-called 'facts' from?

The newspaper!

I suppose that should make me understand his bigoted, ignorant attitude.

The whole thing is completely ridiculous and insulting.

I don't know who was carrying the virus first and neither does he.

And you want to know something? I don't care!

What the hell difference does it make to how we live our lives now?

Stop blaming and start doing.

God knows, there's enough hate and prejudice in the world as it is without us adding to it.

How can I drum it into his thick head that this thing is not about who you have slept with?

It's simply about whether you use condoms or not.

Whoever it was that gave either of us the HIV probably didn't know themselves, and someone gave it to them and they probably didn't know either.

So who's to blame? No one.

People don't intentionally go around infecting other people.

The fault lies in not practising safer sex, in being dumb enough to let a ten minute screw destroy your life.

The bottom line is that we didn't think.

Like millions of other people.

And we just happened to pull the short straw.

Sept 15th

This is all so pointless.

OK, yes, I was naïve too; before I became HIV+.

I thought it was someone else's problem. Not in a million years did I ever believe this would happen to me. Or rather us.

But you've got to move on from that, haven't you?

HIV is not going to rule our lives.

We have a future, a good future.

We're talking up to 15 years.

That's 15 years living, isn't it?

Or is it 15 years dying?

Nov 12th

Mark's gone.

He left me a note this morning.

I can't do anything.

I'm just sitting here like a zombie, trying to take it all in.

He's gone. Left Newcastle, he said.

'I can't explain, I love you too much.' That's what the note said.

I can't take this in.

This is like being told I'm positive all over again.

But worse.

I could have coped if we were going to be together.

I could have been strong for both of us.

This is my fault, I know. Maybe it was me that gave him the virus after all.

I feel tainted, dirty, unclean. If Mark doesn't want me, and my family don't want me, and I can't be truthful with my friends, then what's left?

Suddenly, in one scrappy bit of paper – the back of Saturday's shopping list – the future has melted away. TEN WORDS have made a nonsense of everything I ever wished for.

What's left to believe in?

I understand now why people turn to God.

That or suicide.

I must be somebody really bad to be given all this.

I can't see a point to life without Mark.

Dec 12th

It's a month to the day since Mark left.

And I'm as lonely now as the day he went. Things haven't eased, I sleep with the teddy he gave me, his photo by my side and the pillow is wet with tears.

Dec 15th

Is it really a year since I was told?

Feels like a lifetime.

That's a joke. It is, of course.

I feel a little more OK about it now, not so panicked.

I realise I do have some time left on this planet.

I've been well, my blood count is high, and there has been the occasional day when it's actually slipped my mind.

What's the good news? I got promoted at work, I'm not in the pool anymore, I'm working in Mr McGann's office, in accounts.

He's a really nice man, always says 'good morning' and asks if he wants me working late.

Makes sure I get the overtime for it too, not like Simpson.

He had these travel brochures in the office today. They're going to Tenerife for Christmas.

His wife and their two kiddies.

Can you imagine that? Swimming in the sea Christmas Day, eating smoked salmon and paella instead of dried up bits of old turkey.

Just lying on the beach, soaking up the sun, having nothing to worry about except when you're going to have your next Pina Colada.

Oh, the bliss of it!

If there's one thing I'm determined to do it's that, a holiday in the sun for me and Mark, something to remember.

BEING HIV+

So what's it like having to tell people your status? What worries do you go through both before and after telling them this sort of news?

I asked Maya, who's HIV+ and had to go through it: *My close family, my two daughters' reactions were nothing but kindness and wonderful support.*

I have to say, though, that my sisters were entirely different. They're roughly the same age as me, and they were terrified that their children should find out in case they had any kind of hassle at school, or that it would become common knowledge, and also my sister was totally convinced I'd infected her when I had eaten off the same spoon as her!

This was my sister, who's been a nurse for twenty years.

I can't believe that, what do you mean?
We're talking about Christmas that's just passed. I was eating a piece of cake; put the spoon down. She must have picked the same spoon up and started eating her cake, and then realised it was my spoon.

She didn't say anything at that point; she freaked out about four hours later. She'd been thinking about it for four hours and suddenly she came out with 'You've infected me!' She was screaming at me, and I just didn't know what to make of it. At first I didn't understand it, and then I managed to get her calmed down and she told me what she was on about, and I told her straight. No, I hadn't infected her off the spoon. She didn't believe me; well, luckily I managed to get her to phone up the National AIDS Helpline there and then and have a word with them. She then got really upset because they told her the facts, that of course she couldn't get infected from the spoon . . .

I was really upset. I was convinced then that I lived in this tiny little world which was a small area round my house which was completely protected, but the minute I went outside, into the world, bad things seem to happen because of my status.

HIV AND PREJUDICE

What's so different about this disease that makes everyone jump up and down in horror, start blaming people for being sick and looking on them as members of another race?

It's because we're talking three things here that we just can't cope with at all: SEX, DISEASE (that's Dis-ease ie dis-harmony) and DEATH. Three things that people think shouldn't be talked about in our society.

STOP TALKING ABOUT SEX, DISEASE AND DEATH. YOU'RE UPSETTING THE BUDGIE

Well, this is all rubbish and the only way to raise HIV (AIDS) awareness and change things is to stop the prejudice.

Here's some quotes from some people who've had a taste of it:

Memories ....

Happy days

Must be that
perfume I'm wearing..

Careful. you lot – I had
my hair done this morning!

The deed's been done—
too late to back out now!

Say cheese!

That gorgeous groom –
blushing bride once more!

Mr Fowler...

...and Mrs!

... and a big snog for the camera!

Watch it - this bride's one mean driver

Some people can't even stay awake on their own wedding day!

sharing a jok

Mark is HIV positive:
'*I have a free travel pass because of my (AIDS) diagnosis and I was on this British Rail train.*

Because I'm young, the ticket inspector didn't believe it was mine, he kept saying I must have nicked it.

He kept saying "OK, then what's wrong with you, what's your right to have this pass, you don't look disabled to me."

I told him I had HIV illness (AIDS) and the look on his face was like you wouldn't believe.

He backed out of that carriage faster than lightning.

But he must have told half the people in the train because people kept passing the door and stopping and staring.

It got so bad I had to get off.'

Paul is gay:
'*I told my parents that I was gay.*

My dad said nothing. Then my mum went upstairs and got a load of green towels out of the airing cupboard.

She said that from then on I was not allowed to use the family's towels and could only use those ones.'

Sheila is living with HIV illness (AIDS).
'*I was in my local hospital just recently, for what my GP had called "social care" because I'd had a fire at my house, and I went in there and after about three*

days the nurses wouldn't even speak to me, I thought it was because they were busy, I didn't really take much notice, then they moved me to a different ward, into an obstetrics (mothers and babies) ward which was the only place they had a bed, and I was then confronted by a nurse who asked me if I was a threat to her patients? Was I putting them at risk?

That meant she didn't understand anything about HIV, also it meant that she didn't even consider me to be one of her patients, which really upset me.

In fact, what upset me more at the time than her concern about HIV, was that I was totally excluded from everything, even as a patient!

It made me just think, who was I? What was I?

And I immediately signed myself out of the hospital.'

STAR INTERVIEW

Stefanie has been HIV+ for 7 years. She lives in London, loves travelling, dancing and having a good time and is going steady with a dishy guy.

Have you come across any prejudice?
Loads, loads and loads.

Where do I begin?

I didn't see a dentist for four years because nobody would see me, even in big cities like Liverpool and Manchester I couldn't get one to treat me.

I was being honest with them, I was saying 'I'm positive, I just want you to know'.

When I was living there I phoned up the local group to find out if they had a list of sympathetic dentists and they said well, at the moment we don't tell them because if you tell them they won't treat you and it's very important to keep

I'M NOT PREJUDICED YOU UNDERSTAND BUT WOULD YOU STAY RIGHT OVER THERE AND PUT THIS BAG OVER YOUR HEAD?

your teeth and mouth healthy, so I was actually advised not to say anything. That was the only way I would get treatment, they said they should be protecting themselves against HIV and hepatitis in the normal course of their routine anyway.

But I couldn't do that, why should I have to feel secretive about it?

Another thing that happened was my doctor wrote HTLV3 which means HIV in great big red pen and highlighted it in yellow, and put it on the outside of my medical files. I could actually see it from walking in to the surgery, it was just shining out amongst all the others.

He said he had to do that in case somebody else treated me in an emergency and he wasn't there to tell them.

I was very upset about it, I phoned him up about a year later, when I'd got myself together and he apologised.

The official line is that there's no need for anything on the outside of your files, in fact there's no need for a GP to know at all.

What you can do is say 'I want to tell you this in confidence, I don't want it going in my notes'; make it very clear that you want them to know so that they can treat you properly but you don't want it written down.

I go to my hospital now and I don't have a GP.

There's more. . . .

A friend of mine lost her flat, the landlady found out she was positive, she came home one day and all of her belongings were just thrown down the stairs, she found them in a heap in the hall with a note on the top saying 'We don't want people with AIDS living in this house'.

I know a woman who had to have her baby in a hospital broom cupboard because they wouldn't have her on the ward.

I know loads of people who've lost their jobs when people at work have found out. They've either been hounded out, or it's been made very clear that they couldn't stay.

Any more? The instances of prejudice don't seem to stop, or get any better, I could fill the book.

How would you like to see things change?
I'd like to see an end to this stigma and discrimination.

I'd like to see people who are HIV+ be able to be open about their status.

I'd like society to be tolerant and caring.

I'd like there to be a commitment from the government and from the authorities, a commitment to challenging the ideas and issues around HIV and AIDS.

People can live for 15 years or more, probably more, but we don't have any exact figures at the moment.

You can't spend fifteen years of your life being a victim, being stigmatised.

If people were allowed to be open about their status I think everybody in society would benefit, because they'd see that HIV can affect anybody, that it's got nothing to do with who you are, that's completely irrelevant; this can happen to anybody and I just think that people should open their eyes a bit more and open their hearts.

Suzy Malhotra works at BHAN the Black HIV/AIDS network (phone number at the back of the book), she loves food, reading and French films! Favourite Pastime? Travel and holidaying in hot weather!

What are the particular problems for Asian communities with regard to HIV?
Sexual issues (including those to do with HIV) are not necessarily discussed within Asian fami-

lies, so that makes it quite difficult for people to get the information they need.

Young people in particular have to rely on their schools, that's not always too good either, as some don't cover all the issues.

But organisations like ours are working to provide the right back up, so people have somewhere to go.

Have you come across any prejudice against your members?
Asian communities tend to be very closely knit, and some people feel that if they disclose their positive status they will be shunned by their families and friends.

That is, however, a bit of a myth; if someone is sick they are far more likely to be welcomed and supported by their family than not.

Stephanie was born in Bath, in the West Country, she likes all kinds of music like jazz, soul and blues. She lives in a flat with no pets 'I used to have a hamster, but he died and I'm too heartbroken to replace him!' Favourite TV prog? 'Fresh Prince of Bel Air. Northern Exposure.' Favourite nosh? 'Ackee, saltfish and green banana, oh yes, Roti too, that's delicious!'

Have you come across prejudice?
Of course I've come across prejudice.

Just living as a black person in a white society one is bound to experience this.

Assessments for HIV care and support services are sometimes based on assumptions, not facts, for example when a black person goes to HIV services it's sometimes assumed that they'll want support from a black agency like BHAN which isn't always the case.

Some black people feel more comfortable going to a general agency where there'll be less chance of seeing someone they know from their community.

Again it's often believed that black people living with HIV are part of a large extended family and will automatically be supported. Whilst this is true in some cases we see lots of individuals who say that we are the first black people they have told about their status.

This can often mean that people don't get access to the services they are entitled to.

WHAT TO DO ABOUT IT?

There's loads of stuff to do to change all this
☆ Talk to people about their feelings and try and change them. Write to newspapers and the press whenever you see something bigoted and pathetic. Ring the TV and make a complaint if you see something that encourages prejudice.
Their numbers are BBC 081 743 8000
ITV 071 584 7011

☆ Wear a Red Ribbon all the time. People are wearing these as a sign that they want to support and show care for people with HIV. Organise groups to make them up and give them out. Show people you care.

RED RIBBON

'The Ribbon Project is aimed at showing your commitment to the fight against AIDS.' (*Visual AIDS: American support group*)

If you wear a Red Ribbon you are saying that you are working to get rid of prejudice around HIV and are supporting people living with it.

The ribbons have been made by people both HIV+ and HIV−.

In the same way, some who wear ribbons are positive, some are negative.

Just as with the virus you can't tell by looking who is what.

QUESTIONS AND ANSWERS ABOUT BEING GAY

What's gay?
Gay is people who prefer to have sex with members of their own sex. That's men having sex with men and women having sex with women.

It is true that only gay men get HIV?
No.

People may try and tell you that because the numbers of HIV+ people in the UK seem to be higher in the gay community than in the heterosexual one.

But if one looks properly at the figures what comes out is:

1. *Worldwide, the figures for HIV/AIDS are far higher for heterosexuals than for homosexuals.*
2. *Figures in the West are for HIV illness (AIDS) diagnoses and not for simply being positive. It may be that the virus has struck the gay community earlier so they're more aware of it, and more gays are getting tested.*
   We don't know how many heterosexuals are positive as so few have been tested – we usually only find out they've got it once they fall seriously ill and get an HIV illness (AIDS) diagnosis.
3. *The percentage rates of HIV infection are increasingly rapidly in the heterosexual community, it's not how many have it that is so important, it's how fast it's growing.*

Perhaps we think more about the gay community in terms of HIV because they are the ones who have been so responsible in making us all aware of it. Also I think

heterosexuals like to believe it's only a gay problem because it lets them off the hook.
(Wouldn't it be nice if the gay community were thanked for being so responsible around this issue and acknowledged for the work and care they've shown? Sue)

Is it all right to be gay?
Over to Michael Cashman here. (Michael played Colin in EASTENDERS and did the first homosexual kiss in a TV soap.

The next day the papers were full of hate and horrors. Michael had a bad time from people prejudiced against homosexuality).

'My own reaction is that from a very early age I was attracted to the same sex, I would say from about seven years old.

It wasn't until my early teens that I suddenly learnt guilt.

I learnt that a lot of people around me didn't see what I was doing as right . . . and so I had to start hiding my attraction to other guys and that was what I perceived as WRONG not my gayness.

When you hide your sexual attraction you hide what you naturally are, you become dishonest. . . .

There is nothing wrong with being attracted to someone of the same sex. . . .

What is absolutely RIGHT is that all sex and sexual activity should be consenting (that means both partners really want to take part, Sue).

People shouldn't be forced into anything they are not comfortable with.'

Chapter 6
GILL'S STORY

March 8th

I joined BODY POSITIVE today. It's a support group for people who are HIV+.

I was really nervous going down there, I was so scared people might see me going in to the building and that it would have AIDS stamped all over it. But there's nothing, just a little brass plaque with the number and the address on it.

I was scared about something else too, I kept thinking I might see all these really sick people and I've never met anyone else with AIDS before, or even HIV.

Apart from Mark, that is, sounds stupid, but I didn't know how to speak to them.

In fact all the prejudice I know that my mates would have if they knew I was HIV+ was exactly what I was feeling about so-called 'THEM'.

It took me ages to pluck up the courage to walk down the steps, I felt like I would have to come face to face with my own future.

That said, I knew I wanted to go, I have felt so alone these past few weeks with Mark gone, the flat seems enormous without him here.

March 10th

Guess what, it was nothing like I imagined. If Mark was here now he'd just have shrugged his shoulders and told me off for worrying about nothing.

There were some of the nicest people there, I even saw Laura, a girl I know, there!

I didn't find out if she was HIV+ because she didn't talk about herself and I didn't want to intrude. But I hope I'll see her again.

We had coffee, and people talked about things they were worried about. It was mainly to do with housing benefits, of which there seems to be very little, and whether you tell other people or not.

Two people there go out into the community and give talks about being HIV and how to stop the virus spreading.

This one guy, Philip, said he was talking to a group of sixth form kids and halfway through the kids were going on and on about the press and how it's all a load of rubbish and that AIDS is only in Africa.

That's when he told them he was HIV+ and that he'd got it from sleeping with a girl he'd been going steady with for months, apparently they just forgot the condoms one day, she'd just finished her period so they reckoned they'd be safe from pregnancy, and that's all they thought of.

He told all this to a group of sixth form kids he'd never met before.

Apparently the whole room went silent. And this guy who'd been making really crass remarks about gays and drug addicts and stuff came up from the back and in front of all his mates apologised to Philip and shook his hand.

Philip said that proved how worthwhile it was him telling people about HIV.

I was really shocked. Not shocked in the bad sense but I just think it's amazing that he could be so strong as to do that.

He's only a small guy too, not that that makes any difference. But you'd think he'd be scared of being beaten up or something 'specially at a school in Byker.

His honesty is amazing.

I couldn't do it. I seem to be scared of my own shadow these days.

Still, I'm glad I went though.

May 17th

Haven't seen the family for over a year now.

Rang Mum up the other day. She still hasn't told Dad or Tracy. Doesn't want to upset things she said, it's not quite the right time, what with the threat of redundancy coming up at the yard.

What was it last year? I remember: 'Probably not a good idea to upset Tracy just as she's coming up to her mocks'. I don't know about upsetting Tracy, she failed them all anyway, except for Art.

Then she said, 'Oh Gill, why do you have to bring it up again? Every time we talk you do have to mention it don't you?'

And then she's off, about the new kittens next door, the Irish guy across the road punching in Mr Thomson's front door, how the area is going downhill now the wrong sort have moved in. I can't believe her sometimes.

May 20th

I'm feeling rough at the moment. Can't work out whether it's all in my head or whether there's something wrong with me. And then if there is whether it's down to the HIV or if it's just one of those things.

Something you never think about when you're sick is that it's so boring!!!!

I just seem to be too knackered these days to go out like I used to.

So what do I do instead? Sit around and watch the telly! And what's on telly? Zilch!

I always used to think it was so romantic being sick, even dying of something like leukaemia. I always thought you just got paler and a bit thinner and looked beautiful and a bit sad, draped across some beautiful man in a white nightie.

And what's the reality? Spots and skin rashes and endless trips to the hospital.

August 17th

It's been a bit of a summer. Baking hot again.

I'm being plagued by midgies, covered in bites.

There's this bloke, John, an old friend of Mark's, who won't let me alone.

He's really smitten, though I say it myself.

Keeps sending me little notes at work and keeps mysteriously 'turning up' at lunchtime when I'm having my sandwiches.

He's quite sweet really, and I must say the ego's flattered.

Another time, another place you know.

Sept 2nd

Funny talking about John, I eventually bowed to the pressure, he caught me at a weak moment and I said I'd go out with him.

Because I couldn't think up another excuse in time more than anything else.

And actually, you know he's very nice. I surprised myself, the first time I'd laughed in ages.

Got a bit embarrassing when it came to the goodnight kiss, he took it for shyness so I let it go at that.

What the hell, I said I'd see him next week. You can't be forever moping indoors, can you?

November 2nd

Been back for my appointment at the clinic. Things aren't wonderful I have to say.

It's not that I've had a lot of stuff go wrong. There's been practically nothing, a couple of mouth infections, a bit of trouble with my chest but that's been cleared up now. Nothing much.

I do get tired very easily but I put that more down to Mark going than anything else.

Michael keeps telling me to avoid stress, attend relaxation classes, they do free massage for HIV+ people at the centre. But I can't seem to, I keep looking for signs all the time.

Mark and one of his mega cuddles, that'd sort me out.

Anyway, enough of all that rubbish, apparently my T cell count is dropping.

It's not necessarily significant, because counts can go up or down. But apparently what they look for is a 'general' trend.

By that I think they mean that if it goes down regularly over a period of months it means the virus is getting active and infections might creep in.

Well, the result of all this is that they want me to go on to AZT and come in for fortnightly checkups.

I know he said that would only be at the start, to check how I was doing but two things worry me about that, one is that I don't know how to keep on making excuses at work for time off, I've already been hauled in to the boss twice this summer, he reckons I'm faking it.

If he only knew, I'd be sacked tomorrow.

The other thing is that my doctor is part of a trial, and I don't know if he wants me to go on to AZT because I'll make up the numbers for the trial or if that's what actually is best for me.

You can't really ask for a second opinion because there is only one HIV AIDS specialist centre in the North East.

There's people at Body Positive who swear by AZT, say it's kept them alive years longer, there's others who say the side effects are so bad that it's obvious it can't do any good.

It's difficult to know what to do for the best, there's no one really to advise.

I wish I could talk to my mum about it.

Dec 22nd

I've decided to go to London after Christmas. I don't want to spend any more time up here.

I'm not going to find Mark or anything. It's just that there seem to be more people down in London, more support and a better choice of medical services.

Apparently there's a group called The Terrence Higgins Trust who have people called 'Buddies'. I'm not sure what they do but I think they help out if you don't have any family.

Also I get the feeling that they're beginning to suspect something's wrong at work. Now I'm on the trial it means I have to go to the hospital much more than I used to.

The other day Mr Evans called me in to the office and asked me if there was anything I'd like to tell him, how was I and stuff.

I lied through my teeth of course but he said that if I didn't keep better attendance I would be in line for the chop. He didn't put it like that of course, but that's what he meant. Apparently they have to lose four jobs by the next financial year and he would 'hate' one of those to be mine. So everyone needed to work that 'little bit extra' these days, to keep up the orders and if that meant staying late every now and then well, that's a sign of the times.

Basically what he was going on about was that if I couldn't do overtime for nothing I'd be out. Well, I just can't. A day just about does me.

All I'm good for after that is home and a hot water bottle.

The AZT's done me a world of good by the way. My count is back up high and the side effects haven't been too bad.

I got a lot of sickness at first, and massive headaches, but things seem to have settled down now and I'm feeling quite stable.

Dec 25th

Happy Christmas, diary!

I couldn't face the thought of jolly celebrations with the family and all that.

I told Mum I wanted to stay up here and man the helpline.

She agreed immediately, not a word of protest.

Said maybe it was for the better, she was worried it might slip out, and that she'd be nervous for the children. Didn't want them to catch anything, not that you can . . . 'but you know just in case'. Said she'd tell them I was with my new boyfriend.

I know I suggested it but she could have protested a little bit. Or suggested New Year or something.

I've had a frozen turkey roast dinner and a Mr Kipling mince tart. Pathetic, isn't it?

February 14th

A valentine from John.

Nothing from Mark.

That's decided it.

Laura and I are going to London.

Laura's got a mate who lives in South London – Tulse Hill – and she reckoned there's loads of places going round there.

Says that the Terrence Higgins Trust might be able to find us a place to live.

I think it's a really great idea.

Can't wait to see the back of Newcastle, I'm telling you.

Feb 20th

I got the sack yesterday. And you know what? I don't care!

Old Simpkins hauled me into the office and said how 'sorry' he was but he was just going to have to 'let me go'.

God, the rubbish they speak.

I was really good, didn't say a thing. Just let him drone on and on about 'compulsory redundancy', how 'everyone was cutting back these days', how the orders 'just weren't coming in' and 'ha ha' he was going to have to look out for his own job pretty soon.

I don't care, I heard from Mrs Rabinne a week ago anyway, and so I got all the hurt over then.

What's the point anyway? It was a cruddy job and I'm worth more.

It's strange, you know, I never felt as strong as this before I got the virus.

Living with HIV has really taught me a few things.

After all everyone is going to die one day; I'm beginning to accept that alright, I might go before other people but who knows what the doctors may come up with?

And I really want to live my life now; think about

what I'm doing and why. I don't want to be stuck in some cruddy office, wishing I was somewhere else.

And I'm not going to spend the rest of my life running around after other people thinking they're better than me either, because they're not.

I have as much right to happiness as anyone else and I'm going to start taking it.

Gosh, to see all that written down looks really strange. But I stand by it.

Maybe being positive is the right way round to be for once!

I suppose it shows me how much I've changed.

Two years ago I wouldn't say boo to a goose!

Feb 21st

The one thing I forgot to mention was that Webbers Ltd gave me two months' pay as redundancy which was great.

It's given me enough to . . . guess what? Put down a month's deposit on a flat in London.

And we're – that's me and Laura – moving down there on June 1st!

I don't know if you remember but I met Laura at Body Positive. I saw this girl the first time I went there and thought I recognised her from the club but I didn't get a chance to chat.

Well, it turns out that she was two years above me and she's positive too. To be honest I don't know if I would have had the courage to go back if I hadn't seen her there.

Well, we've become really good mates and so now we're moving in together.

She's been positive for seven years and has hardly been sick at all, which gives me great hope.

She says that she can go and get a telesales job and that with my housing benefit we'll be able to pool our resources. We won't be badly off at all actually, as long as the social don't find out she's living there.

I'm really looking forward to it.

Can't help thinking about Mark though, I know I shouldn't, and I won't go off and find him but I suppose because we'll both be in the same city I can't stop thinking.

That's probably all a load of rubbish, I never stop thinking about him anyway, I just love him too much.

But apart from that, it's reasonable to want to know how he is, isn't it?

Knowing him he'll probably be fit as a pig.

I hope his family have accepted it and been a bit nicer than mine have. I never hear from Mum at all these days. She just doesn't seem to want to know.

March 11th

It's good we're moving to London because I got my AIDS diagnosis today.

It shouldn't matter but it does.

I know that logically I'm the same today as I was yesterday, but somehow there seems to be an awful lot of difference between being HIV positive and having AIDS.

It's like now there's no way out and there's only one road to walk down.

Stupid because that was always the case but it feels different. My head is doing funny things.

I'm working hard here to find something good to say about it.

I guess it means that our housing will come through quicker.

I guess it means now that there's no uncertainty around the illnesses I get, they'll all be HIV related.

Michael, my doctor, said that it's a statistical thing mostly and if I had been in America I would have been diagnosed AIDS last year.

Apparently over there they go on blood counts and if you go below 200 you're automatically AIDS.

I do feel upset though, it's only been four years and somehow I don't feel it's fair.

GETTING THE HIV ILLNESS (AIDS) DIAGNOSIS

An AIDS diagnosis is not the same all over the world. AIDS isn't something you 'develop' or 'contract'. It just means that the point has come when the HI virus has invaded your body to such an extent that the number of disease-fighting cells is way down. Because of this you may also have developed an HIV related illness.

Blood counts measure the number of white T cells, which means they measure how many disease-fighting cells there are in your body. The less fighters you have, the less able your body is to fight infections and disease.

In America they have just accepted a new definition which includes more illnesses and also anyone with a blood count under 200 (a healthy blood count is anything between 500 and 1200 cells).

It may not sound like it but in general this is good news for Americans, because over there people can't get medical help paid for unless they have an (AIDS) diagnosis.

So by widening the definition more people can get the treatments they need and hopefully they will live longer.

What happened before was that people were dying possibly earlier than they should have done because they couldn't afford to pay for the treatments.

Fingers crossed that's never going to happen in Britain.

In Britain you are classed as having HIV illness (AIDS) if you have had any of these and are HIV+.

PCP:	a sort of pneumonia
Toxosplasmosis:	infection of the brain
Cytomegalovirus:	a viral infection that can cause blindness or diarrhoea
Blood poisoning	
Meningitis	
Bone or joint infection	
Kaposi's sarcoma	Skin cancer
Lymphoma	Cancer cells and tumours carried by the lymph system (this is what Gill got)
Dementia	Like senile dementia, the brain's affected so you go a bit dotty
HIV wasting syndrome	Slim disease, lots of vomiting and diarrhoea making you thinner and weaker

These diseases are serious but can be treated. But the more affected someone is, the more open they will be to future infections.

Should you worry that getting diarrhoea or thrush or flu is a sign you might be HIV+? No, absolutely not. We all get ill from time to time, it's a part of life. What we're saying is that people who are HIV+ get these diseases like everyone else – but in their case they don't have the immune system to shake them off as a healthy person can, and they can get seriously ill.

THE AIDS DIAGNOSIS – DO WE NEED IT?

As we've mentioned, an AIDS diagnosis depends on a series of different things.

But how does it make a person feel?

I DON'T WANT TO TALK ABOUT IT I DON'T WANT TO TALK ABOUT IT I DON'T WANT TO TALK ...

I think it's really rough. Think about it.

First you get told you're HIV positive. That is an enormous thing to take in, and very frightening and life-changing to start with.

Then you may get symptoms and a variety of infections, and that's pretty worrying.

Next, what? Some doctors will give you an ARC diagnosis (AIDS Related Complex), that means you're on the way to AIDS.

How does that make you feel, OK because you've not yet got AIDS or worse because you're past HIV?

Next you get the AIDS diagnosis itself.

People have told me that having that is like being told you're HIV+ all over again.

Does it have to be like this?

Isn't the term HIV+ enough?

I think having the term AIDS as well just makes people more stressed, and it's been proved that stress is an important factor in staying well or getting sick.

In fact a lot of doctors are thinking like this now and it's reckoned that pretty soon the word AIDS will be faded out.

QUESTIONS AND ANSWERS ABOUT THE (AIDS) DIAGNOSIS

How long is normal between contracting the virus and getting sick?
In brief, it's 6–10 years in the West (that's Europe, the US and Australia) with the right medicines. In the developing world (that's poorer areas like Asia, Africa and South America) it's a different story. Because of poor health care and people being in less good shape to start with, the average is more like two years.

HIV POSITIVE? TAKE TWO ASPIRIN AND HAVE A GOOD NIGHTS SLEEP

When does the AIDS diagnosis happen?

When you've had one of the infections outlined above.

This doesn't mean that people who've been diagnosed AIDS go on being sick for the rest of their lives.

It's more likely that there will be periods of time when people feel well and live normally.

They may get infections which would then be cured. What it does mean though, is that the person with HIV illness (AIDS) is more likely to go down with a disease which over a period of time will weaken their body.

Neil has been living with HIV illness (AIDS) for three years now:

How does it feel to get an AIDS diagnosis?

Horrible. And scary. Like being diagnosed HIV all over again. You have to go through the whole thing of coming to terms with it all over again.

Do you see a doctor regularly, do you have to?

I don't have to, but I do.

I see a consultant every three months just to have blood taken, have the tests done, more for my own peace of mind than anything else, I want to know what's going on in my body. What's going on with the immune system really.

Do you take any medication at all? Antibiotics or whatever?

I take prophylaxis, a preventative for PCP, which is Septrin. I take it on three days of any week.

I was taking the nebuliser (inhaling vaporised medicine through a mask) but I found I was very allergic to it. I had to take it for two weeks out of every four but I found my nose got very sore. I was walking around with a big red nose for half my life so I stopped taking it.

Chapter 7
GILL'S STORY

March 22nd

I'm writing to you from a new address. Get this:

26 Pindar Grove, Tulse Hill, London SW17 8EU

It's a sweet little flat and exactly 8.8 miles from Walford (I looked it up), and who lives in Walford?
I know, I know, and he's probably off with some other girl now and we haven't got a hope. But what have I got to lose?
Let's face it, I don't want to spend what's left of my life alone, and right now I look OK. It'd be much better to make contact now when I'm well; and I am going to get sick, I have to accept that.

Remember that dream I had of going abroad with him, I'd like to do that.
Anyway he doesn't have to see this, he's never going to know and what else can I dream about?

March 31st

Laura and I are well settled in now.
It's a great flat, quite small (we share a bedroom) but a separate sitting room. It's in the basement of

this lovely old house, and the kitchen has got french windows leading out on to a patio.

I went to Woolworths today and bought some climbers to grow up the walls, honeysuckle and a clematis with big purple flowers.

Then some roses which are supposed to have this lovely scent. I've got my bits and pieces all around, Mark's photo by the bed, it's beginning to feel like home.

April 22nd

I have to say there's not a lot to do round here, unless you go into town that is, and everything's so expensive!

Just the tube fares knock you back. And that's before you've had a drink.

The clubs charge you to get in and the price of drinks on top makes going out a Saturday night event only!

I've got a little job, shorthand and typing as a temp.

It suits me brilliantly actually, because they just ring up day by day and I don't have to declare it.

And of course, on the days I'm not too good I don't have to go in.

Haven't plucked up the courage to go to Walford yet, I really want to but then I'm really scared that Mark is just going to ignore me.

I want to leave it till I'm well, also until this rash clears up.

I know it's only my vanity but I've had shingles and it makes my skin look all dry and scaly and I just hate it.

Some days I look really old.

So I'll have a few days off and then when I'm OK I'll go and see him.

Wish I had a phone number for him, or even an address.

In all that time we were together he never let on where he lived, just talked about 'ALBERT SQUARE'.

Hope it's not a whole district or something.

I'd kick myself if I didn't at least try.

May 28th

Well, I got it together and went and saw him.

It was real luck actually, I noticed that the 437 bus from the high street went all the way to Walford.

Never mind all that stuff about getting dolled up and that, I was outside Boots and saw this bus and just thought what the heck?

After all, it isn't as though he hasn't seen me looking ordinary.

In fact, he'd laugh at me if I suddenly appeared all glammed up on a Wednesday afternoon.

Well, I got there and almost backed out. I had to go and have a coffee and a cream bun (great for my figure) before I got the courage up.

I asked this bloke on a fruit stall if he knew of anyone called Mark Fowler.

He pointed up the street to what turned out to be Albert Square.

I was just turning this corner when I saw them. My heart froze, there was Mark and this girl, with the most beautiful long blonde hair you've ever seen, mucking about in the square.

They looked really happy, laughing and joking.

Well, I should have cleared off right then. (Mum always said I never know when to call it a day), but it was like I was fixed to the spot, I just couldn't do anything 'cept watch them.

Mark put his arms round her, they went into this big clinch and then he saw me.

May 30th

What happened after that?

You want to know, don't you?

Why do I do this?

He's seeing a girl, that girl, the one I mentioned with the blonde hair, she looks really young, her name's Diane and she lives practically next door to him.

Though I hate to say it, she seemed quite nice.

I know I should have expected it and I did, but there's nothing like a bit of reality to smack you in the eye!

They seemed so in love.

How can men just love?

When I said I loved him I meant it. Love means wanting to be with someone for the rest of your life.

It means sharing things through the bad times as well as the good.

Doesn't it?

Or did a little bird tell me wrong somewhere?

I told Mark I loved him and that means . . . it means I'm not going to go careering off with some other guy if things get a bit complicated.

That's a joke, HIV is a bit more than a complication, but you know what I mean.

And we're both in it together.

He's HIV too, it's not just me and this bloody virus.

Or maybe it is. That what it feels like sometimes, I'm telling you.

So what does he do?

Clears off without a word, he did, he just disappeared, I told you that, didn't I? I came back from Webbers, I remember, it was a Tuesday, and he'd gone.

A note to say Sorry, Gill, I've had to go, I can't explain, I love you too much, Mark.

No address, nothing. Well, he's proved how much he loves me, hasn't he?

I don't want to go on any more.

What's the point?

FACTS ABOUT BEING HIV

✶ ✶ ✶ ✶ ✶ ✶ ✶ ✶ ✶ ✶ ✶ ✶ ✶ ✶ ✶ ✶

STAR INTERVIEW

Patrick is 21 and due to HIV illness has to spend a lot of time at home. He has lots of hobbies like swimming and reading, and has a part-time job, three hours a week at the local Body Shop.

Patrick has just started on his gold Duke of Edinburgh award organising a charity football match.

How is it, day to day, for you?
Life is very unpredictable. One day I can be feeling fine and the next I can be so tired and breathless that I have to go on my oxygen.

I have treatment once a fortnight in the form of an IV infusion/drip.

This gives me replacement antibodies, which means I get a bit more immunity to help fight infection.

How does it make you feel? Coping with all this?
I do get depressed from time to time, more out of frustration than anything.

I see my friends going out and getting themselves full-time jobs, passing their driving tests, going abroad on holiday and just having

the independence and freedom that comes with youth, and I get very angry that my illness restricts me from being like them.

Sometimes I just wish I could walk away from the illness and live a normal life even if it was just for one day.

So what are the symptoms of HIV illness (AIDS)?

I guess what's important to know is that when you have AIDS more and more of your time is taken up with being sick, in pain, going to hospital for treatment and feeling weak.

It's very difficult too, to keep happy, all your mates out enjoying themselves. There's enough to cope with feeling down and not well. On top of that there's a lot of prejudice around.

This is awful and makes me very angry.

BUDDIES

Like Gill, some people living with HIV illness have very few people around to care for them. It may be that the family can't handle the situation or that their friends are frightened or far away.

It may be that the person feels they don't want to impose on family and friends.

In that situation they can ask for a buddy. This is someone who is prepared to help in any way they can.

The THT (Terrence Higgins Trust) trains and runs buddy groups and matches buddies to people with HIV.

STAR INTERVIEW

Jenny has been a buddy for three years now; she has buddied four people with HIV.

Jenny lives with her girlfriend in Cardiff. She works part-time as a filing clerk for Rank Xerox.

Why did you decide to become a buddy?

When I started buddying I was only working part-time and so I had quite a bit of extra time on my hands. It was about the time when we first started really hearing about HIV in this country, and quite frankly all that 'information' was starting to freak me out a little bit!

I decided that the best way to deal with it was to confront it, literally, to try to understand first-hand what the reality was.

Does it take up a lot of your time?

It can take up an ENORMOUS amount of time, depending at what stage the person who's ill is at.

When that person is relatively fit and well, it may be just a weekly visit and perhaps a daily phone call. But if someone is seriously ill you may be taking phone calls at 2am, visiting all the time, supporting family and friends, and trying to fit in the rest of your life around an impossible schedule.

The pressure mounts up at this point and it is essential to get support from your own BUDDY GROUP, always there to help you through the crisis.

Having said that, time takes on another dimension in these special circumstances, and I would say don't even THINK of becoming a Buddy if you are not willing to GIVE time and MAKE time.

Have you any happy memories of people you've buddied?

YES! YES! YES! Absolutely! The level of sharing and communication can become very intense; compared to an ordinary friendship that builds up over a number of years, you find yourself compressing experiences into a much tighter time frame.

These experiences have a sort of 'edge' to them; you laugh harder, you cry harder.

Once I rushed to hospital to visit Brian, knowing that his body temperature had dropped and that they had had to cover him in foil to keep the heat in. When I arrived he had scrunched all the foil up and wrapped it around his head like a turban! I think he was meant to be Carmen Miranda! You just remember these moments and a very warm feeling comes over you. There are MANY happy memories, too numerous to mention.

How do you talk to their families?

Families may not always understand or appreciate you being there; you have to be very patient!

You have to try to put yourself in their shoes, know when to back off to let them share quiet time, know when to make a cuppa, know when to give them a hug.

There are no written rules here; you rely on your instinct and common sense totally, to feel your way.

Are there any funny or peculiar moments you can remember?

Once, Martin decided that he wanted to go shopping in South Kensington. He was very wobbly on his legs but we decided to give it a go. Writing out the shopping list made us laugh for a start. . . .

1. *Carton of carob flavoured soya milk*
2. *Fresh king prawns and tabasco sauce*
3. *Extra large Y-fronts.*

He often experienced strange food cravings (and compared himself to a pregnant lady), and the Y-fronts were for what he called his 'bony bum', a result of losing weight.

He leaned heavily on me during the whole trip, and though he was exhausted he kept his sense of humour at all times . . . even when people looked at us like a couple of old drunks.

If only they'd known how brave he was.

Do you have to take precautions when looking after someone who is HIV+?

I give hugs and kisses freely and have never felt funny about it. Everyone knows by now that outside of exceptional circumstances there's only ever a real risk when an exchange of body fluids is involved.

Human contact is vital to communication; fear is always recognised on a deep level and the person would pick up on this.

Common sense at all times and in large doses!

Were you ever scared of not coping with what was happening?

Yes. When I did feel that, I was just feeling overwhelmed.

I also worried that Ian (who I was buddying) didn't like me and that I was disappointing him in some way. It was irrational but I couldn't see the wood for the trees!

Finally, after some great support from my group, he asked for me very late one night in hospital to tell me I was his 'knight in shining armour'. It made me feel very small, very humble, and deeply touched.

If you are interested in becoming a Buddy, you can phone the Terrence Higgins Trust for details.

You DO have to be 18 or over, but 'the most important thing is that you have a non-judgmental, non-discriminatory attitude and a respect for confidentiality.' Telephone 071 831 0330 and ask for a Buddy Liaison Officer.

If you're not yet 18 there are still lots of things you can do, so call them to check it out.

Chapter 8
GILL'S STORY

Jan 3rd

Another year and I'm still around.

Things are sorting out, life seems to get calmer for me now.

Of course I still have great bouts of panic and depression but I feel more understanding about it.

I don't want to fight any more, to stand up and hate the world.

I've given up blaming myself and other people for this thing called HIV.

It's a part of my life, not my death, and I am learning to live with this invisible creature called the virus.

It's a long time since I've written this diary, over 6 months.

I did see Mark once or twice after that incident.

But he's still so angry and upset.

Said he'd been to see a counsellor with Diane.

Some stupid nancy guy, he said.

I find it hard to understand his attitudes.

I can't see how it makes it any better for him to deny it all the time.

Once you have HIV, that's it. You can't go backwards, you can't make it 'unhappen'.

It seems to me that by pretending it doesn't exist you're just going to make it more difficult in the long run.

Also, medically it doesn't seem too good an idea.

If you don't go and see a doctor there's no way they can keep a check on your health.

If you don't know whether you're healthy or not you aren't going to get the treatments you need.

And if you don't get treatment you're going to get sicker quicker.

Not hard to work out, is it?

Well, I decided I didn't want to be around all that.

Too much to cope with as well as my own problems.

It's funny, although I still love him to bits it's like a part of me has grown up and he's just stayed where he was all these years.

They say men never grow up, don't they?

Well, I guess men living with HIV aren't any different from all the other sorts.

Jan 15th

We've decided to have a New Year's Eve party. Only we didn't get it together in time so it's going to be next week instead.

It's amazing when you go down the list how many

people I've got to know in London, not all from Body Positive either.

All in all it'll be about thirty people. Not bad for only 6 months here, is it?

Goodness knows how they're all going to fit into this tiny place. I'd thought we'd be adventurous with the food, go a bit more upmarket. We've decided on a Mexican theme so there's going to be a big bowl of Chile con carne and rice, and tacos and tortilla chips.

Laura said she'd make a guacamole (is that how you spell it?) I haven't a clue what it is, she says it's something to do with avocados and yogurt, or is it aubergine? I don't know. I've probably got it all wrong, I'd never even heard of an aubergine before I came down here.

Sounds impressive anyway, I can tell all me mates like I've been doing it for years, as long as I check out how to say it.

The tacos are easy, you get them in Safeways down the road.

Then we're supposed to be having this Mexican punch. I ask you, where are you supposed to find what goes into that?

All I know about Mexico is that there's a lot of desert and men on donkeys wearing sombreros.

Jan 23rd

This is one very sleepy Gill writing in this diary, but I just had to write this before I crash out.

Mark came to the party, I didn't know he was coming, didn't even know Laura had invited him.

I suppose if I'm really truthful, I was secretly hoping but I just didn't dare to.

It's incredible but after all these years and all he's done, I'm just as much in love with him as ever. They say that there's only one person in your life, that you truly deeply love and I know that's true. And I know it's Mark.

What can I tell you?

We just talked and talked. Practically the whole night, and the time just slipped away. He's looking really good and says he's had no problems.

Told his parents, they seem to want to ignore it all, rather like Mum.

I suppose the bad news is that he's got another girlfriend.

Why do I have to love someone so attractive?

Apparently she's called Rachel and is really clever; teaches at a college or something.

He's moving in with her, so I suppose it's pretty serious. We could have been so good together. I still don't understand why he had to go away, it doesn't make things any different, does it?

We said we'd keep in touch. But I don't know if he will. I have to be strong about this and leave it up to him. Hope he does though.

Feb 11th

I've had such a smashing day.

Went over to Walford to see Mark and we went bowling. God, I haven't done that in ages.

He's still as useless as he always was. I beat him 189:121.

Afterwards we had a fish and chip supper on the back of the bike.

It was smashing. I haven't laughed so much in ages. Also, his thing with Rachel seems pretty much over. Not that there was all that much to it in the first place anyway, or so he says.

Apparently she's really intellectual and everything has to be an issue. Has to have a reason to it. He says they never just have a laugh.

Well, it's the opposite with us, I don't think we've ever discussed anything serious in our lives, apart from the HIV stuff of course; well, that's not true, because he avoids that as well.

I've got butterflies in my tummy.

Feb 22nd

Mark's been stopping here for a few days.

He had a big row with Rachel and has decided to move out.

It's been lovely having him here, feels like old times.

Only thing though, his sister Michelle turned up. He'd told his mum and dad but not her.

I cleared off, went to pick up my prescription and then wandered up and down the High street for two hours until I thought it was safe to go back.

I don't know what went on because he won't tell me but now he's suddenly decided that he's going to move back to Newcastle and he wants me to go with him.

I have to say I hate Newcastle, what did it ever do for us, except split us up?

It'd just be a load of unhappy memories.

Still, he's behaving like a bull in a china shop as usual. Not giving himself time to think. Maybe he'll change his mind.

I don't know whether to try to talk to Michelle or not, I've only met her twice but she seemed really lovely and she must be feeling pretty devastated.

Left out too, like everyone knew but her.

March 18th

Mark's here for good (fingers crossed) and I love him, love him, love him.

I knew it'd all work out alright in the end.

We're just made for each other and however hard he might try to deny it, well, we just can't.

I started my new regime today:

NO TOXINS!

There's a lot of proof that it works. It makes sense, doesn't it? If you keep on shovelling rubbish into your body, it's not going to behave.

So ... boring, boring, it's no meat, no sugar, no alcohol and, of course, no nicotine.

A high-fibre, high-protein diet to boost the immune system.

I've got this book on it from America and the writer has been living with AIDS for ten years now!

Can't be bad, eh?

And my immune system needs all the help it can get right now, my T count is down to 115.

In a lot of ways I think it's better not to know, but at this hospital it seems you've no choice 'cos they tell you anyway.

Not that that means anything necessarily. I'm sure that what is most important is how you feel.

My doctor, Mary, says it's OK too, as long as I don't lose any weight.

Well, I'm not exactly skinny now, so I don't think there's going to be any problem about that.

No, I really feel I'm on top of this thing now.

I've had no illnesses for ages, my medicine is fine and I feel brilliant. Never better. I have more energy than I've had for years. Guess it's Lurve!!!!!!

March 31st

Mother's Day.

I sent Mum a card.

With my phone number on it. I'm on my own in the flat. Mark's gone off to see his. I'm thinking about that little baby of Sarah's. He'll be four now.

Expect he'll have done her a drawing for Mother's Day.

April 16th

I've been reading this brilliant book about 'existentialism'. The idea is that if you do an ordinary thing in a completely different way from the way you normally do it then you will see it in another light.

And if you do this with everything you do, what will happen is that your mind will begin to look at things in a new way. Things that were ordinary before will become exciting and wonderful again, like they did when you were a baby.

Do you get it?

Well, I have to say I didn't really either, but I thought I'd try it anyway, see if it worked.

Mark thinks I've gone absolutely potty but I think it's brilliant.

It's made me feel really good and has put away all those horrible scares about the sickness coming back that I went through last month.

We went to Albert Square to give Pauline an Easter egg and I met some wonderful people.

There's a brilliant lady called Dot, she went around making beef sandwiches for everyone, just because she felt like it.

And I saw Rachel again. And some of his mates. The square is covered in daffodils right now and looks just beautiful.

Life is good, I have to say.

April 30th

Well, Mark's got a place of his own now.

A squat above Sam and Ricki's.

It's fine and I'm not worried or anything.

The flat's so small and dear Laura has been ever so patient, but it must have been difficult for her, not knowing when to come in or whatever.

The squat is quite nice actually, much better than you'd think. I reckon it needs a lick of paint and some of our things around but it could look cosy in no time.

I can't help hoping that it will be our little flat. I haven't dared ask but he has given me a key.

And Tulse Hill is ever so far to get back to late at night.

Keep your fingers crossed for me.

I have to say I hope he'll be there if things get bad. I don't expect he will, he's always been squeamish like that and as I well know he's not one for facing up to things.

Trouble is, I haven't got anyone else.

Ah well, maybe it won't come to that, not for a bit anyway.

May 12th

STUDIO
SCENE 753/12 INT. SQUAT UPSTAIRS. DAY (13.15)
(*IF THERE'S A SOFA GILL LIES ON IT. IF NOT SHE'S LYING BACK IN A CHAIR. THE CURTAINS ARE CLOSED. MARK KNEELS BESIDE HER, STROKING HER FOREHEAD.*)

MARK: You ought to see a doctor.

GILL: I've got a headache.

MARK: It's not just a headache.

GILL: Believe me, it's my head, it's just a headache.

MARK: Please go and see a doctor.

GILL: Please don't bully me.

MARK: I'm not bullying you. (*Pause*) OK, I'm bullying you. I'm sorry.

GILL: (*Smiles*) I've just taken some more aspirin, it'll go away soon.

May 13th

I've been feeling a bit off recently, over a week now. Headaches like you'd never believe. Much worse than when I first started on AZT.

Sometimes I lose vision or go really dizzy. My reactions seem slower too, I'm writing this and having to think about every word I write.

It's very strange and I don't know what's happening. I'm a bit scared too, is this the start of something else? Mark keeps telling me I should ring the hospital, but I don't want to, not just yet, in case it might be something.

I have a sensation, like I know there has been a big change in my body.

I don't think things are very good.

I think maybe I'm going to get sick now.

I don't want to say goodbye. I'm too young for that. Aren't I?

I do hurt.

STUDIO
SCENE 753/5 INT. SQUAT UPSTAIRS. DAY (10.00)
(*MARK'S IN HIS LEATHERS AND PREPARING TO LEAVE. GILL, IN NIGHTDRESS WANDERS THROUGH FROM THE BEDROOM*)

MARK: I'm sorry, I didn't mean to wake you up.

GILL: You didn't. Have you got anything for a headache?

MARK: There should be something in the bathroom. Top shelf, left-hand side.

GILL: Thanks.

MARK: What's the matter?

GILL: Nothing really, just a man with a pneumatic drill hammering inside my skull.

MARK: I could call in sick if you like, stay here with you.

GILL: I've got a headache, that's all.

MARK: OK. How about meeting some-where for lunch? Covent Garden perhaps?

GILL: It's a bit of a trek.

MARK: The Vic?

GILL: OK.

MARK: About one?

GILL: Fine.

MARK: You go back to bed.

GILL: Yeah, I think I will. Top shelf, left hand side.

MARK: That's it. *(Kisses her)*. See you lunchtime.

(Mark leaves. Left alone, Gill sits in a chair holding her head and grimacing with pain)

May 14th

STUDIO
SCENE 754/18 INT. SQUAT UPSTAIRS

MARK: Where have you been?

GILL: To the zoo.

MARK: The zoo?

GILL: I just fancied it somehow. I've never been before.

MARK: The zoo? In Regents Park?

GILL: Actually I didn't like it much. There was one of the big cats, a panther I think it was, I'm not sure, it was pacing up and down. I thought, I know just how you feel.

MARK: Have you been there all this time?

GILL: More or less.

MARK: You could have left me a note or something.

GILL: *(Pause, then suddenly angry)*
               Oh, Mark, I'm so angry. I'm trapped
               in this body, there's nothing I can do
               . . . Yesterday it was a headache, and
               what's it going to be tomorrow? Flu?
               Pneumonia? What? There's nothing I
               can do except wait and get angrier
               and angrier . . . it's not fair. . . . It's not
               fair . . .

               (Mark holds her as she sobs)

May 26th

I'm sitting here in bed at St Mary's. Mark has gone
home and I'm so frightened.

I don't think I've ever been so frightened in my life.
We came in really early this morning. Been up all
night with these awful head pains, like blinding flashes
you wouldn't believe.

Couldn't do anything but be sick and stagger
about, they've stopped it now and I feel doped up
but at least the pain is just a throb now.

And they give me stuff whenever I feel it's coming
back.

She said they are going to do tests. They've found
something.

A lesion on the brain.

You can go mental with AIDS, you know.

You can get something that makes you blind; that

scares me more than anything else I think, not being
able to see the day.

I wish my mum was here.

LOCATION
SCENE 758/11 INT. HOSPITAL WARD   DAY
11am

GILL: I had the strangest dream about you.
             You were talking to me, only at a
             distance, right? And when I asked
             how you were able to do that, you
             said, 'I'm on the psychic telephone
             line.'

MARK: I was, too, I was sitting there at
             home, trying to send you messages.

GILL: What messages?

MARK: Well, the main one was . . . yeah, but
             you know, don't you?
             (Gill shakes her head)
             Yeah, you do. Three words. Eight
             letters.

GILL: Say it.

MARK: I can't, I'm too shy.

GILL: I love you.

MARK: Yeah, that's the one.

LOCATION
SCENE: 758/17 INT. HOSPITAL WARD   DAY
1.15pm
(Gill is putting on her makeup. Mark sits at her bedside watching her)

GILL: Is this too much?
               (Mark looks at her)

MARK: Bit much eyeshadow.
               (Gill wipes some of it off)

GILL: I want to look good. I want to look so
               healthy she'll have no excuse for
               keeping me in any longer.

MARK: Gill, if she says you should stay in . . .

GILL: She won't. I'm fine now. OK, my
               head was sore, but it's better.

MARK: Yeah, but . . .

GILL: What?

MARK: Well, they did give you a shot of
               morphine.

GILL: All right, so what if they did? All that
               proves is that there's nothing wrong
               with me a shot of morphine won't
               sort out, doesn't it?
               *(Gill starts to apply her lipstick, we
               see that her hands are shaking, she*

suddenly smears the lipstick across her cheek)
Drat it, oh, what's wrong with me? What's wrong with me?
(Mark takes a tissue and tries to wipe the smear from Gill's face. Gill suddenly looks scared again)
Mark, you know about the dementia?

MARK: Keep still, the what?

GILL: You can get dementia with AIDS.

MARK: Yeah, I know.

GILL: What if this is the start of it? What if I'm going to lose my mind?
(Mark shakes his head, upset at the idea, and unable to find words of reassurance)

GILL: I'm not very brave, am I?
(Dr Atkins looks round the door. Mark and Gill look at her apprehensively)

LOCATION
SCENE 758/19 INT. HOSPITAL. THE WARD. AT GILL'S BEDSIDE. DAY 1.35pm.
(Gill is staring blankly at the doctor)

DR ATKINS: Lymphoma. Non Hodgkins Lymphoma to give it its proper title.

GILL: Oh. And what does that mean?

DR ATKINS: It means that you're very seriously ill
              indeed.

GILL: I see. And how ill's 'very seriously ill
              indeed'?

DR ATKINS: In your case Gill, I'm afraid that
              you're not going to get better.

GILL: *(Pause)* I'm going to die then?

DR ATKINS: I'm sorry, but the answer has to be
              yes.

GILL: How long. . . ?

DR ATKINS: You might still have a few months.
              (Pause)

MARK: Surely that can't be it? Surely there's
              something you can do for her.

DR ATKINS: We could treat the lesion with
              radiotherapy, that might certainly
              slow down its further development.

GILL: Would that give me longer to live?

DR ATKINS: It might. There's no guarantee.

GILL: I see.

MARK: Well, you've got to try that Gill,

haven't you? You've got to try any
treatment that's going.
*(No response from Gill. Mark
appeals to Dr Atkins)*
Hasn't she?

DR ATKINS: I think we should let Gill make up her
own mind on that, Mark.

GILL: This is all very strange.

DR ATKINS: I know. I'm sorry not to have better
news.

GILL: It's all right. It's not your fault.

DR ATKINS: Gill, if you need to talk to someone, I
can arrange for one of the counsel-
lors to see you.

GILL: It's OK, thanks.
(Silence. Then Gill says)
Can I go home now?

May 30th

I'm tired, so tired.

Yes, and all the other things, like fear and
loneliness and pain. There's a lot of that these days.

Mark is still insisting I take the radiotherapy. I can't
see the point of it myself.

I mean, what is the point?

I can't remember what she said, but even if I go through all that it will still be something else. And sickness and no guarantees.

Is there a purpose in life if all you're doing is waiting for the next lump of pain and fear to come along?

I don't want people to go on seeing me like this. Getting worse and worse so they have to do every little thing for me.

I never thought I was a proud person but maybe I am. I want to be left with a little dignity.

Please.

18th June

It's not all bad, you know. The days are beautiful now, warm and sunny, the birds singing all day.

This little flat is very special.

I am trying to remember it. To note down all our things. Our times we shared.

I know now it's time to go to the hospice. I'm too sick and it's not right for Mark to have to see this.

Illness is so basic, mopping up sick and messing the bed.

It's almost like your body goes back to being a baby, there's no control any more. I seem to loll about too, can't keep my limbs in order, or maybe that's just the drugs.

The love I have for Mark.

I so want to give him something. To leave him part of me.

It's stupid, I know, but I can't get out of bed to go and find it.

Wish I'd thought of that before I got so sick.

Well, if you ever read this, Mark, I love you so much. There would never have been anyone else, I know that even if I'd lived to a hundred.

I'm sorry we didn't get to share the things we should have done, even the bad times, like the rows. They were never really that serious, were they?

They never stopped what I felt for you.

I'm sorry we never got to share some children, to watch them grow up. I would have liked that. Can you imagine a little one? I bet he'd have had all my stubbornness and all your temper.

Maybe it's for the best after all.

All I ever wanted out of life was you. And a couple of kids.

That's all.

They say you think it's never going to happen to you but I guess it had to happen to someone, didn't it?

Mark, don't see your future in me. Don't worry.

You're well and you're strong. They'll find a cure.

I love you so.

SCENE 764/28 INT. MARK'S SQUAT [NIGHT 10.45 pm]

GILL: Would you do us a favour, Michelle?

MICHELLE: *(Smiles)* Name it.

GILL: Will you brush my hair for me?

MICHELLE: Yeah, I'll do that. Mark's not the hairdresser type, is he?
              (Moves to get hairbrush)

GILL: No, no, he's not, but . . .
              (Michelle returns with hairbrush. She gently brushes Gill's hair)

GILL: Michelle.

MICHELLE: Yeah?

GILL: Look after him for me?

MICHELLE: Don't worry about that.

GILL: I don't just mean now. I mean later . . .

MICHELLE: I know what you mean. I'll be there.

FACTS ABOUT HOSPITALS AND HOSPICES

Here's an extract from a letter written to me by Russell. He looked after his partner Sandy, for the last three years of her life.

Like Gill, Sandy decided not to go on with treatments after a certain point. That can be very difficult for the people caring, if they want more than anything else for that person to go on living, even in a way that is so limited because of their illness.

'. . . *During all the time I had with Sandy, I never once faltered. When she was sick I cleaned it up. I never failed, if she made a mess, of herself or her bedding, I cleaned it up, I never failed.*

Sandy was my life and everything she did made me love her more. I wanted Sandy to marry me, and I asked her every day of the three years we had together.

It was not all mess and cleaning, we had lots of good times, we watched and loved each other more every day.

The hardest thing to do was to watch Sandy reject all the doctor's advice. I believed she knew what she was doing. So we just carried on the way we were.'

THE LIGHTHOUSE

After all the depressing side, I've got some good news. It's not all misery. For example, there's a place in London where people can go and stay for 3–4 weeks at a time.

It caters specifically for people with HIV illness.

THE LIGHTHOUSE IS BETTER THAN A FIVE STAR HOTEL BECAUSE HERE YOU DON'T HAVE TO LEAVE A TIP

I went there to visit a friend the other day and I have to tell you it's lovely, not like a normal hospital at all. There are some single rooms and all of them are fresh and bright with flowers and comfy chairs.

People are offered a variety of therapies which include massage, acupuncture, counselling and aromatherapy.

The most important thing is that the Lighthouse puts power back in the hands of the patients: it's up to them to take their medicines, have a shower, get ready for bed. There aren't rules and regulations that are enforced; anything and everything can be talked about.

There's a creche where mums can take their kids, visiting is any time of the day or night and there's lots of workshops going on.

If someone dies they light a candle for a week in their memory.

They always need volunteers so if you want to help, give them a ring.

• •

THE NATIONAL AIDS HELPLINE IS ALWAYS THERE AND IT'S FREE. THEY WILL HELP ON ANY ISSUE TO DO WITH HIV AND AIDS.   0800 567123.

• •

THE MILDMAY HOSPICE

The Mildmay is a centre which has residential beds, a drop-in centre, and day support for people living with HIV.

People also go to spend the last part of their lives there.

It's a place of calm and peace.

There's a balcony filled with scented plants, a fun bathroom with bright tiles and ducks and toys and they've just opened a new wing which is specifically for mums and their kids.

You can get alternative therapies there as well as counselling.

The people at The Mildmay helped me a lot when I was researching the part of Gill in EastEnders. Before that time I had only seen people healthy with HIV. It sounds morbid but when Gill was diagnosed with the lymphoma, I needed to meet and talk to people in the last stages of their life.

I went to the Mildmay and spoke to some fantastic people.

One of the guys, Malcolm, died three days after I spoke to him.

He was very thin, so thin I was nervous to touch him in case he'd break.

He told me what he wanted at his funeral, the songs he wanted played: Bette Midler's 'Wind beneath my Wings' and Elton John's 'Song for Guy'.

Like Gill he didn't want many flowers, he wanted the money instead to go to HIV/AIDS charities.

He wasn't a religious person so instead he wanted people to stand up and say anything they felt like, a poem or a bit about something they'd shared; whatever.

Malcolm, we miss you.

What's the difference between a hospital and a hospice?

The most basic difference is that a hospital tries to cure you of illness and disease.

This can involve you in treatments that are painful or make you feel bad, like radiation therapy for cancers.

In a hospice, all the care is given to making you comfortable and free of pain, rather than trying to cure you. Any drugs and treatment you receive will be to make you feel better and more comfortable.

Hospices can really help a patient prepare for death in a calm and peaceful frame of mind.

SUPPORTING A PERSON WITH HIV ILLNESS (AIDS)

What's the best way to give care and support to people living with HIV illness?

You know, perhaps the most important thing is being there. Living with HIV illness (AIDS) can at times be the most frightening and lonely thing. Knowing that someone is there at the end of the phone or coming round to see you can do as much as all the medicines put together.

People need support and there are lots of ways to do this. The person needs trust, confidentiality, love and friendship.

They need a lot of information about the problems they might face and how to cope with them.

Regular visiting or phoning is important. Always arrange it, don't just turn up. An illness causes tiredness and sometimes a visit can't be coped with.

Talk about the illness if that's what's wanted. Many people feel angry and feel better if they have someone they can be angry with.

Sometimes people will want to talk and sometimes they'll want to ignore it. Try and listen to how they are feeling by letting them do the talking.

Share outings and arrange visits to other people. Simple trips to the shops, for example, can be good news if you've been stuck in bed all week. If you go away keep in touch by writing or phoning.

Some emotional effects of HIV illness (AIDS) might be:

Extreme stress or upset

Feeling anxious about the course of the illness
Feelings of powerlessness and loss of control
Not knowing what will happen
Personality changes: loss of memory, confusion,
anger, depression or fear
Guilt about having the disease
Worry about family or friends

Some social effects of HIV illness (AIDS) might be:
Dependence on others
Rejection and loneliness because of other people's fear and prejudice

Is it right that doctors should tell people when they're going to die?

Over to John here. John is a senior nurse counsellor caring for people with HIV illness:

'I don't think it's appropriate to tell someone how long they've got to live, because there's a very good chance they'll programme themselves to live for that particular period.

People who are told they've only got three months for example, WILL probably only live three months; it's a sort of self-fulfilling prophecy that I've seen happen a number of times.'

ACCORDING TO THE
COMPUTER YOU HAVE
3 YEARS, TWO DAYS,
4 MINUTES AND 10 SECONDS
TO LIVE

DOCTOR

How does it feel to be really sick?

Mike:

Rotten!

I am, I believe, in the last stage of my life here, and most of my days I am confined to bed.

I get frustrated because I want to do so much, and my body won't allow it.

Taking a walk is an effort these days, it's the same with sleeping and eating.

I am tired a lot of the time yet I can't sleep for long.

I am not scared of dying, I just feel sad that I have achieved so little in my life.

Sarah:

It's boring because you can't do anything except wait and hope you might feel better.

I'm not scared of death, I think it's just part of a natural progression on to something better. My illness has to be for a reason and it can't be so that when my time does come, I will go on to more suffering or complete emptiness, there has to be something better to progress on to to make sense of all this illness.

FACING TERMINAL ILLNESS

Most people, especially young people, go through a lot of different emotions when faced with a terminal illness: FEAR, ANGER, GRIEF, RESIGNATION AND ACCEPTANCE.

Part of the acceptance bit is coming to terms with what's happening, and a lot of people do that by trying to sort things out.

That means things like: seeing old friends and saying goodbye, resolving arguments, getting rid of possessions and furniture that is not really necessary, writing a will, or doing something that's really important, like Gill did with her marriage.

GETTING RID OF UNNECESSARY OBJECTS

Some people with AIDS like to plan their own funerals (as Gill did), to choose how they will say goodbye to friends and family. This is not morbid, it's just another way of accepting what's going to happen.

Susan, a friend of mine, sorted through all her belongings and gave something special to each person that she knew.

Raj, a friend of mine, gave each person a tape of his message. Another friend made a video, of themselves and their close ones, using a camcorder.

BARNARDOS has produced a 'memory box', where people can put little personal things like letters and trinkets, so the special people left behind will have something of them.

Chapter 9
GILL'S STORY

June 21st

It's beautiful here at St Mary's.

I was very frightened when I first came in. I seemed to be losing control of my body more and more.

The fits, the vomiting, bedwetting and diarrhoea.

It's humiliating, made me feel so ashamed, and so helpless not being able to control it.

And the pain kept coming back, too fierce even to reach out of bed to get the pills sometimes.

So I knew it was time and it was a good thought because here all is different.

The room is lovely, a window to see the birds and George, my nurse, has put a birdtable outside my window.

We had a squirrel come for the nuts this morning. Mark has brought me freesias, my favourite flowers and the room is full of their scent.

And George ... George is my nurse and he used to be a trawlerman in the North Sea.

He sits on the edge of the bed and tells me stories, like we've all the time in the world, and at some moments, you know I almost believe it.

The pain is gone, George showed me how to

prepare for when it comes back, and to take my pills before that happens.

I'm left feeling sleepy and yes, a bit weak but not angry.

I'd like it to be over soon.

Maybe my family will forgive me then.

June 23rd

LOCATION
SCENE 765/2 INT. GILL'S ROOM AT THE HOSPICE. DAY (9.30am)

GILL: Thanks.
            (George stands, picks up tray. He is just about to exit when there is a tap at the door)

GEORGE: Let yourself in.
            (Mark enters, bearing his bunch of flowers)
            They're nice.

GILL: *(Smiling)* Hi. Come on in. George, this is Mark.

GEORGE: *(Grin)* Yeah, I know, we met the other day. Sit yourself down and I'll bring you some coffee and a jug for those.
            (He exits, Mark approaches Gill, kisses her)

MARK: How are you?

GILL: *(Smile)* OK. *(About flowers)* They're beautiful, thanks.

MARK: I got them because they were smelly. *(Little laugh)* Thought they'd knock out the smell of disinfectant.

GILL: There isn't one.

MARK: *(Mock stern)* I didn't know that! *(Looking around room)* This place is more like a hotel than a hospital.

GILL: It's good. *(Indicates towards door)* He's great, that George. He was telling me he used to be on the boats. You know, trawlers and that.

MARK: Yeah?

GILL: Till he developed *(painful giggles)* an allergy to haddock. *(Pause)* Oh dear, I shouldn't laugh, it hurts.

MARK: It's nice to see you smile.

GILL: He's funny.

MARK: I can see I'm going to have to watch you with him.
           (Gill smiles, holds his hand)

GILL: You do that.

MARK: I'm serious. I'm not having you flirting
           with every ex-trawlerman who hap-
           pens to catch your eye.

GILL: Oh, yes? And what are you going to
           do about it?

MARK: *(Pause)* I think I'd better marry you.
           That'll stop your nonsense.
           *(Gill's smile fades. She downcasts her
           eyes)*

MARK: Will you marry me, Gill?
           (She turns her head away)

GILL: *(Low, upset)* Don't be ridiculous.

MARK: Why's it ridiculous?

GILL: *(Pause)* You know perfectly well
           why.
           (Mark turns her face to him again)

MARK: *(Soft)* I know why you think it's daft —
           (Shrug) we'll just have to agree to
           differ. I repeat, will you marry me?

GILL: *(Whisper)* I can't!
           *(Mark is unfazed. George taps on the
           door. Enters with new tray of coffee
           and jug of water)*

GEORGE: Shall I come back later?

MARK: No, it's OK.

(George ignores him. Sets tray down. Goes to Gill)

GEORGE: *(Pause)* You OK, sweetheart?

GILL: Yeah.

MARK: I just asked her to marry me and she turned me down.

GEORGE: What?
(Gill less upset, but a little sour)

GILL: It was a nice thought, though.
(George looks shrewdly between them. Questions Mark with his eyebrows; Mark nods. George speaks to Gill)

GEORGE: Don't you love him?

GILL: *(Surprised)* Yes, but—

GEORGE: Then in that case, you're mad. Good-looking oik like that and you're turning him down? You're out of your mind.

GILL: *(Astonished laugh)* George!

GEORGE: *(Stern)* Do you love him?

GILL: *(Pause)* Yes.

GEORGE: Would you LIKE to marry him?

GILL: Yes, but—

GEORGE: Good. Now then. *(Stern to Mark)* When were you planning this extravaganza?
(Mark extracts the receipt from his pocket, shows it to George)

GEORGE: Right. Now let's start again and this time we'll do it properly. *(Pointed, to Gill)* And there is no problem that can't be sorted, all right?
(She smiles. George turns to Mark) Well, go on then.
(Mark. Happy but rather embarrassed)

MARK: For the third time of asking – will you marry me?
(George looks expectantly at Gill, who smiles)

GILL: Yeah, OK.

SCENE: 765/6 INT. RACHEL'S HOUSE. DAY [10.45 am]

MICHELLE: *(Thunderstruck)* You what?

MARK: Me and Gill's getting married this afternoon at three o'clock.
(Michelle sits heavily)

MICHELLE: *(Flat)* You are kidding, aren't you?

MARK: No, I got the special licence last week.

MICHELLE: But why?

MARK: *(Shrug)* We love each other.

MICHELLE: Mark, she's dying!

MARK: *(Loud)* I know! So if we put it off, there won't be time, will there?

MICHELLE: *(Pause, gentle)* I'm sorry, I didn't mean to sound *(Pause)* you sure about this?

MARK: *(Low)* Yeah.

MICHELLE: *(Small smile, sigh)* Oh, Mark!

MARK: I know it sounds crazy *(Pause)* but you tell me what's sane in anything at the moment!
           (Michelle looks at him, thinks about this)
           I'll tell you what's sane. Making sure someone knows you love them, that's what's sane. Making sure they're not on their own! Making that sort of commitment even if it's only for five rotten minutes!

LOCATION
SCENE 765/8 INT. GILL'S HOSPICE ROOM. DAY.
(10.55am)

(George is sitting on Gill's bed fixing her up to the syringe driver)

GEORGE: Comfy?

GILL: Yeah.

GEORGE: OK. This beastie will give you a constant feed of medicine through-out the day without you doing a thing.

GILL: What is it?

GEORGE: *(Grin)* A syringe driver. Basically, it pumps in a brilliant cocktail of pain-killers, this, that and t'other – in the best case it will buy you a pain-free, trouble-free wedding day.

GILL: *(Slightly apprehensive)* And in the worst case?

GEORGE: *(Matter of fact)* In the worst case, you might have a fit every half hour. In which case, you still get a worry-free day, because George will be right there beside you to sort it out.

GILL: *(Surprised)* You're coming to the wedding?

GEORGE: *(Laugh)* I'm not letting you out of my sight, young lady. In fact, you're very lucky I don't insist on being best man.

GILL: *(Quiet smile)* I'm glad you'll be there.

GEORGE: *(Smiles)* Me too.

MICHELLE AND MARK IN THE SQUAT PACKING GILL'S CLOTHES IN A HOLDALL

MICHELLE: There, that's about it, I think.

MARK: Thanks, Michelle.

MICHELLE: *(Pause)* Have you got a ring?

MARK: A what?

MICHELLE: A ring. You know the thing you're supposed to put on her finger.

MARK: Oh Lord, I'd forgotten about that.

MICHELLE: *(Pause)* Never mind.
            (Mark starts going through his wallet. He is too distracted to notice Michelle taking a ring from her pocket)

MARK: No, it's OK, I've just about got enough to – I mean, it won't be a good one but – oh god, how could I forget about that? Look, 'chelle, could you lend me a few quid so's—
            (Michelle holds the ring out)

MICHELLE: *(Quiet)* Oi.
            (He looks up)

MARK: What's that?

MICHELLE: *(Pause)* My wedding ring.
               (Mark just stares)
               Go on, take it. I'd like to see it going
               into a good marriage.

LOCATION
SCENE 765/12. EXT. HOSPICE GARDEN. DAY
(12.00am)

MARK: *(Alarmed)* Why can't I see her?

GEORGE: *(Gentle)* She doesn't want you to.
               (Smile) What self-respecting bride
               wants to be seen preparing for her
               wedding?

MARK: *(Still concerned)* Is that all?

GEORGE: *(Gentle)* Mark, time's too short to
               mess around. She's resting, she's
               collecting her thoughts, she's prepar-
               ing to sparkle at her wedding. If it
               was anything else I'd tell you.

MARK: *(Reluctantly convinced)* Yeah, OK,
               thanks.
               *(George leads Mark to the seat. They
               sit down)*
               George. . . ?

GEORGE: Mm?

MARK: Am I doing the right thing?

GEORGE: *(Considering rather than pat)* Yes, I think so. And more to the point, so does Gill. *(Smiling at Mark)* It's made her very happy, and that's the right thing in anybody's book.

MARK: Has it? Has it made her happy?

GEORGE: *(A little laugh)* Oh yes. *(Pause)* She was very concerned that it was a selfish thing to do, marrying you knowing she'd make a widower of you so soon; but then she decided she wanted to do it to please you.

MARK: *(Taken aback)* Please me? I was trying to please her!
(George looks at him. Smiles)

GEORGE: Yeah, well, wouldn't it be nice if all marriages set out in that frame of mind *(Pause)* Eh?
(Mark takes this in)

MARK: Hadn't thought of it like that. Can I ask you something?

GEORGE: What?

MARK: You deal with it every day, people dying. *(Pause)* Doesn't it ever hurt?

GEORGE: *(Simple)* Yes.

MARK: Then why d'you do it?

GEORGE: *(Pause, smile)* People come here to
               die, Mark. They're frightened,
               they're in pain, they're anxious about
               their relatives, all sorts. *(Pause)* Each
               person that I can help to die painless-
               ly and at ease; each relative who's got
               an ounce more heart for tomorrow –
               (Little laugh). Well, it beats trawling
               for flatfish, I can tell you that.

LOCATION
SCENE 765/22 INT. REGISTRY OFFICE. WED-
DING ROOM. DAY (3.28pm)
TUESDAY 23rd JUNE
*(The Registrar stands behind the table. Mark, Gill,
Rachel and Michelle in front of it. Gill looks happy but
tired; Mark actively supports her with an arm around
her waist. At the back of the room stands George
with his wheelchair, beaming.)*

REGISTRAR: *(Smiling)* . . . and in the eyes of the
               law I now pronounce you man and
               wife.

June 23rd (10.00pm)

Mark,
    I love you, I don't want to say goodbye,
                Goodnight. . . .

                              Gill

Chapter 10
GILL'S STORY

25th June

LOCATION
SCENE 766/9 EXT. HOSPICE. DAY (9.45am)
(An ambulance is parked outside the hospice. Its tail doors open. The ambulance men emerge with Gill on a stretcher, followed by Mark. They all enter the hospice.)

SCENE 766/13 INT. GILL'S HOSPICE ROOM. DAY (11.00am)
(Gill is in bed, apparently unconscious, George is smoothing out the bed. Tucking her in. Calm, serious, murmuring quietly to her. Mark is prowling furiously, angry and desperate)

GEORGE: *(Low)* There we go, that's better. Everything's all right now; you have a good rest. *(To Mark)* This could be it . . .

MARK: What's happening now?

GEORGE: She's just resting.

MARK: What're you doing?

GEORGE: *(Smile)* I'm making her comfortable.

MARK: *(Loud)* Well, that's no flaming good,
            is it? She's sick. She needs her pills.
            Do something!

GEORGE: *(Low, gentle)* I'm sorry, Mark,
            there's nothing else to do.

MARK: *(Angry)* Don't be ridiculous, there
            must be!
            (Looking wildly round the room)
            Give her an injection or something —
            put her on a life support system.
            There must be something you can
            do!

GEORGE: *(As before)* Mark—

MARK: *(Furious)* What do you know! Flam-
            ing nancy nurse! You don't know
            what you're talking about. I want a
            proper doctor! Who's in charge
            here? Go and find me someone who
            knows what they're doing! *(Tight
            beat)* All right, I'll find someone
            myself!
            *(He makes no move to go. George
            takes him gently by the arm, leads
            him outside into the corridor)*

GEORGE: Mark, Gill can still hear you.
               (Mark stops, turns)

MARK: *(Beat, whisper)* I have to do some-
               thing!

GEORGE: *(Soft)* What you can do is come back
               in and sit down. Chat to her nicely —
               tell her you love her — see her off
               gently.
               *(He shepherds Mark back to the bed,
               sits him down. Makes him take Gill's
               hand, smiling encouragingly. Mark,
               nervous, embarrassed, lifts Gill's
               hand, kisses it)*

MARK: *(Low)* Sorry about that sweetheart.
               (Little laugh) You know what I'm like
               in the morning. *(Pause)* Everything's
               OK now.
               *(He looks to George for reassur-
               ance. George smiles, nods)*
               Love you, Gill, I'm glad I met you. . . .
               *(Gill opens her eyes, manages a small
               grin, whispers as though tired)*

GILL: *(Pause)* It's been great fun, hasn't it?

MARK: *(Pause)* Yeah.
               (Gill closes her eyes, still smiling a bit)

GILL: Yeah.
                *(She takes a deep breath. Seems to
                settle into sleep. Over fifteen
                seconds or so her breaths become
                shallower with increasing pauses in
                between until there are no more
                breaths at all. Mark looks to George)*

MARK: *(Pause, low)* Is that it?

GEORGE: *(Gentle)* Yeah. *(Pause)* That's it.

Sept 1st

Dear Gill,
*I was never very good with words when we were
together, so I don't suppose I'll be much better now;
don't think I've turned into a poet overnight.*

*I actually feel a bit stupid writing in the back of
your diary, and I really hope you don't mind, but so
much of what you've written is about us and in a
strange way, I feel closer to you like this than at any
other time since you died, almost as if we are talking
together once more.*

You have gone, haven't you?

*Every day my first thought as I wake is that I won't
see you that day, and it's really hard to make myself
get out of bed.*

Everyone says stuff like 'Life goes on' and 'Time

heals the pain' and I nod and say yes, but when I'm alone the tears still come easily.

Night times are the worst because I can't switch my brain off.

'What brain?' I can hear you say!

How I miss your wicked sense of humour, how I miss you!

I do have good days (like when I don't think of you for thirty seconds), and I always smile at your photo next to my bed, which is the last thing I see before I put the light out.

Funny that, that's just what it feels like, like a light went out.

It was good fun, wasn't it? That first night in Newcastle when we talked nearly all night and felt like we'd known each other for a million years? Those quiet times at the flat, just you and me.

And at the very end, when there were no more words to say, just holding hands and looking into each other's eyes.

Looking for an explanation, a miracle, anything but what we were going through.

Your diary stops so suddenly that it hurts, I keep wondering what you might have written next. Would you have been proud of me? I tried so hard to be brave for you, you were always strong enough for the two of us, I used to turn away and bite my lip to stop the tears coming and hope you'd never notice.

There are so many things I wanted to say, but time ran out for us, didn't it?

All I really want to say is that I still love you as much as I ever did, and that our love made me strong to face whatever the future brings my way.

I don't suppose anyone will ever read this, and like my memories of our too short time together, I'll keep it safe.

Always with my love, Gill,

Mark X

Chapter 11
FILMING GILL'S DEATH ON EASTENDERS

When you're an actress playing a part there comes a time when it's really difficult to be apart from the character you're playing.

Filming the two final episodes of Gill's life (the wedding and the death) were special in that sort of way.

Firstly, we had the top team on the job; the senior EASTENDERS producers, one of the top EASTENDERS writers and the best technical team.

Next, it was done on location, with only a few members of the cast, so we wouldn't be distracted by the rest of life at Albert Square.

We filmed throughout the weekend on what is called a 'Double Bank'.

This happens twice a year on the programme and it means that four episodes are filmed in a week instead of two. It's so that everyone can have two weeks off at Christmas.

As I said this was a special time, with everyone working hard to create the right atmosphere.

I slimmed down to play the part, losing half a stone before the filming, also my wedding dress was made two sizes too large so it made me look really thin.

It took an hour each morning to do Gill's make-up, and Kate, our make-up designer, did a lot of research to check that she would get it right. She talked to nurses about how people with Gill's cancer look when they are that sick, she consulted books and medical journals and then, before we got to the actual filming, she did a practice run.

During filming she took photos all the time so she could match the make-up perfectly when needed.

For example, Gill put make-up on for her wedding. Well, it's pretty difficult to get the right balance between the make-up for her illness and that to make her look attractive.

But Kate managed it and did it brilliantly!

We had a medical team on hand all the time to help me walk properly and react in the right way to the drugs.

I hadn't had a close experience with someone in the final part of their lives so I needed to know how to portray it, and also how to die.

Gill had 80% paralysis on one side of her body by that time and you have to learn to hold yourself very differently.

There was a piece in the filming when I had to laugh, and I couldn't do it without the 'paralysed' side of my body reacting. We tried and tried but eventually Todd had to hide the persistent muscle twitch by putting his arm round me and covering it up!

In the wedding scenes I felt strange, and had little idea of 'acting' or what was coming across on the camera.

Todd and I were so close by this time that we didn't think about it at all, we just did it, and our director, Leonard, was wonderful, he just let us be ourselves.

All those scenes were hardly rehearsed and were almost all shot on one take.

When it came to Gill's dying, I had to be taught how to change my breathing and how to relax completely.

Apparently you can't really do it, because when you die everything goes, so every muscle relaxes. This just isn't possible in a living person.

After we'd filmed the actual death, the director said CUT and everyone just stayed completely silent.

It was like a moment in time, hanging in the air.

Then I got out of bed and cried, not loud but I couldn't really stop.

Mike, our real doctor, came over and we left the filming. We walked around the grounds of the hospital; it was a beautiful warm spring day, and I had my nightie on and we just walked and talked, of death, of faith and the spring sunshine.

We were away for a long time and nobody hassled me or said a word.

Leonard (our director) just let me have that time. (That's very special because in television there is never enough time and it costs a lot of money to keep people longer.) But that's the care they showed for me and Todd and the rest of the cast.

When I came back it was fine. I had to do some more scenes where she was in the bed and there's a good little 'cheat' that they did to stop me breathing. Underneath the bedclothes, they put a 'cage' of chicken wire over my chest and put the blankets over that. So when I breathed I didn't move the sheets and you can't see it.

I think both Todd and I got a taste of what it must be to lose someone. That weekend will always stay with me.

The week after that, I had to go back into the studio to film part of an episode from two weeks before, when Gill was still sick and deciding to go into the hospice!

That felt a bit funny, and of course I was laughed at something rotten ('risen again, are we?' all that sort of thing), but it was good because it got me back into the real world. Gill was just a part, and now I could get on with the rest of my life.

Except that I found the rest of the nation had been watching the story on television, and some people didn't want to let go of it. Here is just a small selection of some of my real-life experiences at the time of playing Gill:

I was slapped in the face while walking in the street and called 'a filthy whore'.

My son Joe had a Christmas circus event at his school, and I was selling snacks. At each performance several people said 'Don't buy a hot dog/crisps from her, you'll catch AIDS'.

I was in the supermarket doing the shopping and this guy came up, tipped over my trolley, spilling all my shopping on the floor. He shouted 'Clear the store, everyone leave the building, you're in danger, this girl has AIDS.'

I received letters telling me 'the wrath of God' was upon me and I was being punished for my sins.

I received letters telling me I deserved everything that was coming to me and that I was encouraging young people to be sinful.

This is how it was for me, and I was only an actress playing a part! What about real people living with HIV?

I was very shocked at first to be on the receiving end of this kind of prejudice. I felt it was aimed at me personally, but my shock quickly turned to anger and sadness. I realised that people often say hurtful things not because they mean them, but because they don't fully understand the situation, they feel nervous and frightened about it. All this sounds pretty gloomy and depressing, but let me tell you of some of the more unexpected and wonderful moments too!

A lady was following me down the street. I started to feel a bit nervous and walked faster, but then she called out to me so I stopped . . .

She told me that her brother had just died of HIV illness in Ireland and that all the time he had been sick the family had refused to see him.

After watching EASTENDERS on the telly they went to the hospital, hugged him and talked with him, sorting out all the quarrels, finally making their peace with one another.

She believed this had allowed them all to say a proper 'goodbye'.

I was with my son Joe visiting his grandparents and we were feeding ducks down by a big lake.

A couple came up to me and talked at length of how the gentleman had lost his first wife as a result of Lymphoma, the same way Gill had died. He talked and talked of the lovely memories he had of her, and of the happy times they shared together.

People stopped me in the street this way many times, talking of people they have lost through illness, and I've realised that grieving for someone you love binds us all together, whatever that illness may be.

Joe and I were at the Science Museum and a guy came up to me, put his arms around me and wept.

He said it was the first time he'd cried since he'd lost his partner three years ago.

I got on a bus to go to town, the driver stopped the bus in the middle of the main road, horns honking, people getting out of cars to see what the holdup was, the lot; and he wouldn't go on till I'd signed autographs, shaken hands with the whole bus, hugged and kissed one and all.

A mum who is HIV+ and has a seven-year-old said she was able to use EASTENDERS to talk about HIV with her daughter, she'd never been able to tell her before.

Many people living with HIV told me of their experiences and how HIV affects them and their families and friends. Some you will read in this book, for others the experience hurts too much to write it down.

Many are too frightened of the prejudice and hate they fear will come their way if they are too 'open' about it.

I could go on, but maybe it's enough to say that I listened to many different voices and heard a different story from each and every one. I heard about hate and fear, I heard about love and support, I would find myself frustrated one minute, moved to tears the next.

Only the other day, I was walking in Piccadilly where these workmen were doing the road: they called out to me (like they do) and I smiled to myself and walked on. Suddenly, this hunky 6-foot fella leapt out of the hole they were digging, and started to tell me of his girlfriend, she was in the Mildmay (a local HIV/AIDS hospice) approaching the last stages of her life.

He was so worried about coping with their little boy, carrying on working and trying to 'be there' for his girlfriend when she died.

We went for a coffee together and ended up covered in mud and tears!

By the time you read this, Marie will be gone.

STAR INTERVIEW

Todd Carty needs no introduction he's been on our screens for ever, first in Grange Hill, then Tucker's Luck and now EASTENDERS.

Sue: What did it feel like filming the scenes with Mark and Gill?
Todd: For the first time in a long time, I was really touched by something I did in my acting career.

I remember when we were doing those scenes.

And it was, you know . . . it was just all the crew, all very hushed and quiet.

I remember from the very first time of the read-through, people were going 'gulp', you know, holding their breath, because it was so well written. And we just sort of . . . did it. I suppose there was a sort of daziness because we were there all together just constantly for about two or three weeks.

It just became about you and me, about two people loving each other and going through an illness.

You know some people go through the method and some say they are affected by the work they do and some say they aren't, but I can't . . . I don't know of any other bit of work I've ever been involved in that I've been affected so much by.

It's easy to say, 'Oh, I don't have any emotions about this or that,' but . . . I did.

People say 'Why?' I say, 'Well, I did. There was just something about it. You know it was like a love story and we got married and then you went away'.

Sue: Was the filming difficult?

Todd: I remember at the time both of us were very . . . almost you could sort of touch us and we'd sort of spark off something or tears would come, and you know the crew were the same too.

That left a very deep effect on me, there's no doubt about that.

Sue: More generally: what would you say to someone in their first sexual experience. They've got to the 'knickers on, knickers off' bit and one wants to do it and the other doesn't? What does the person that doesn't do?

Todd: The person that doesn't do?

Sue: OK, OK I can't speak English, go on.

Todd: Well, I'd say if they don't want to do it they shouldn't have to.

The pressure being what it is, you know, I mean if it's the guy, in particular of my experience, he doesn't want to do it and he's got to think about his mates and 'Did you do it? Did you do it? Did you do it?' And he might lie and say 'Yeah'. That's OK, but I would say personally, you know, don't do it.

Sue: What about condoms?

Todd: Well, there's all different sorts, aren't there? Flavoured ones – banana and raspberry

and that kind of thing. But the important thing is safety, so always look for the kitemark.
[that's the British Safety Standard mark that will appear on each condom that's been properly tested to a high standard – it looks like a little kite.]
Condoms are simple, but there's not always a lot of information about how to use them. It's easy really, like putting a polo neck sweater on; you just sort of roll them down.

Practise on your own.

Sue: And then when you actually get into the situation, it's not so difficult. Or maybe the answer is to admit it can be difficult for both people and make a joke of it.
Todd: Yeah, exactly, if you're sort of easy about it. And you can actually talk about it. Because you know, there's those little pressures again.

If you can relax about it, and you're quite honest with your partner, you can say; 'Jeez, this isn't working; let's try another one'. You know, something like that. Because they're there to be used and they're one of the only things around for safer sex.

Sue: And maybe not have sex when you don't really want to?
Todd: Yeah, you know, sometimes if you're not in the mood and one partner might want . . . you know, it might be the old headache syndrome, for a man or a woman.

Hopefully I'm as virile as the next man, but sometimes, you know, I might have a headache too. It's the same.

STAR INTERVIEW

Sue Tully plays Mark's sister, Michelle, in EASTENDERS. She lives in North London, is an Arsenal supporter and can whistle the signature tune of every major series on the BBC!

Me: At the moment you're single. Has HIV changed the way you feel about relationships?

Sue Tully: Oh yeah, definitely. It's a completely different ball game now, because I wasn't used to thinking about safer sex; all of a sudden it became an enormous issue to me, you know, and . . . um . . . it hasn't been as difficult as I thought. All the embarrassment I thought surrounded it all, well, that just hasn't applied to me. I don't know but I think the message is getting through and it's, well . . . in the experiences that I've had, it's just . . . a natural part of the process.

I think I've been quite lucky with the choice of partners because I've felt quite comfortable talking about it and so did the guys. The good that has come out of it is that you get to know somebody a lot better before . . . well, I do, I get to know somebody a lot better before I take that step. So by the time I do take that step it's a lot nicer and a lot of the tensions that would be around just aren't there.

Me: Is it difficult for girls?

Sue Tully: For my girlfriends . . . no, it gives them a sense of control and a sense of strength. Not a sense of power because that can be a bit of a dodgy thing, but it's like 'Look, this is the way I'm going to do this and if you're (the guy) intimidated by the fact I'm carrying them (condoms) then I don't want to know anyway.' You sort of sort out the wheat from the chaff quite quickly with this whole HIV issue, I think. Because you cut down to basics very quickly, my girlfriends don't have a problem with it, they sort of enjoy it.

Me: If you could change things in regard to HIV, what do you think would be the most effective thing we could do:

Sue Tully: Chuck money into research as far as I'm concerned. You shouldn't have to rattle tins, it's ridiculous. They can find millions to promote the most stupid things, I won't get political, but this country's got to get its priorities sorted as far as I'm concerned and health has got to be number one. AIDS, HIV is now part of our lives, it's part of our culture now. When you get to meet people it's there, it's on the agenda already. And I think you should build on that, it should be on everybody's agenda all the time.

Me: Do you know how to put a condom on?

Sue Tully: Right, first you have to get into the condom pack itself. Right, there you go . . . Right, now, where's the little dooby? There it is. . . . You want me to put it on this? (a make-up bottle)

Me: Yeah, put it on this. . . . What do you do then?

Sue Tully: Right . . . well . . . you must remember to pinch the top so there's no trapped air, then you . . . roll it down and that's it! Easy!

Me: That's quite easy really, isn't it?

Sue Tully: Yeah. You got one of those Femidom things here?

Me: Yes, we have.

Sue Tully: Have you? Because I'm wondering what . . . I want to see what they look like . . . Oh, there you go.

Me: They're big.

Sue Tully: They're BIG.

Me: And half of them stay outside.

Sue Tully: Well, you see that's um, yeah. . . .

Me: And apparently they're noisy.

Sue Tully: Oh no!

Me: When you're doing it.

Sue Tully: Really? I suppose you'd have to blast your Luther Vandross up then to drown that out.

Chapter 12
THE FUTURE

OK, so we've done the business.

By this stage of the book it's really clear how to prevent HIV from spreading.

It's clear what's safer and what's definitely UN-SAFE.

There's still one BIGGGGGGGGGGGGGG problem.

NOBODY'S DOING MUCH ABOUT IT!

So apart from taking responsibility for yourself, what is there to do?

And the answer to that is MASSES!!!!!!

●●●●●●●●●●●●●●●●●●●●●●●●●●●●●●●

FACT: 2 or 3 people on average die from HIV illness in the UK every day.

●●●●●●●●●●●●●●●●●●●●●●●●●●●●●●●

WHAT CAN I DO?

You can help. AIDS and HIV belongs to all of us. Accept that and do something about it.

CARRY A CONDOM with you always. If you don't need to use it give it to someone who does.

Treat people living with HIV and AIDS with respect and equality.

Work to educate other people

Join a support group or become a peer co-ordinator.

Organise awareness events locally in schools, youth clubs or colleges.

It's up to you and me and every single one of us.

That's the only way we're going to stop our friends from dying.

It's up to us, not someone else or governments, just you and me.

STAND UP AND BE COUNTED!
WEAR YOUR RED RIBBON WITH PRIDE
AND TELL OTHERS WHAT IT'S ABOUT.

BECOME AN ACTIVATOR

There are loads of ways you can do this:

★ Set up an HIV AWARENESS DAY in your workplace, school, college. Get a group of people together and organise an event. The National AIDS Helpline will give you a local contact to find out how.

★ Organise a fundraising event and donate the profits to an HIV organisation. CRUSAID and BAR-NARDOS, for example, are always doing brilliant things and the more money they get the more things they'll be able to do.

★ Become a PEER CO-ORDINATOR and start educating others. Write to the Ibis trust for information on how to get started. (details in back of book)

★ Become a volunteer at your local HIV organisation or hospice. Ring the National AIDS helpline to find out what's needed in your area.

★ Wear a Red Ribbon all the time. Organise groups to make them up and give them out. Show people you care.

★ Talk to people about their prejudice and change it. Write to newspapers and the press whenever you see something bigoted and pathetic. Ring the TV and make a complaint if you see something that encourages prejudice.
BBC 071 743 8000   ITV 071 584 7011

★ Buy safer sex products or gifts from HIV organisations. That way you can support the charities involved. See address section for who sells what.

★ Plan an event for WORLD AIDS DAY which is December 1st every year. The National AIDS trust organise this for the whole country. Ring or write to them at the address in the back of this book.

ALWAYS WEAR A RED RIBBON. GIVE ONE TO A FRIEND. TELL OTHERS WHY YOU ARE WEARING IT AND WHAT IT MEANS.

IT'S UP TO YOU AND ME AND BETWEEN US WE CAN CHANGE THINGS FOR THE BETTER. IT'S NOT ABOUT THEM – IT'S ABOUT US.

Some great one liners on safer sex!

SAFER SEX: What's your position on it?
PRACTICE MAKES PERFECT: SAFER SEX
SEX POSITIVE
RESPECT YOURSELF – SAFER SEX
IT'S NOT WHAT GROUP. IT'S WHAT BE-
HAVIOUR
Your biggest sexual organ is between your two ears –
USE IT!
CONDOMS ARE FOR LIFE
Low Risk isn't No Risk
Condom Sense is Common Sense
Get him to put it on, not put you off
It's not on if it's not on
Getting the virus depends on what you do, not who
you are

Can you think
of any more?

THE NAMES PROJECT

People all over the world have sewn panels in memory of someone who has died of HIV illness. These panels all together make up a beautiful quilt which, sadly, is growing bigger every day.

There are special groups all over Britain that get together to sew the quilt.

It's a way of saying goodbye to the person you've lost and can help your sadness.

Practically everyone that dies from this virus is cremated so it can be a good substitute for the comfort that people get from visiting a gravestone.

It is a permanent, tangible reminder of that person.

If you'd like to find out more, the Names Project UK is at:
86 Constitution ST Edinburgh EH6 6RP   031 55 3446

ALWAYS CARRY A CONDOM WITH YOU. EVEN IF YOU DON'T USE IT YOU CAN ALWAYS GIVE IT TO A FRIEND.

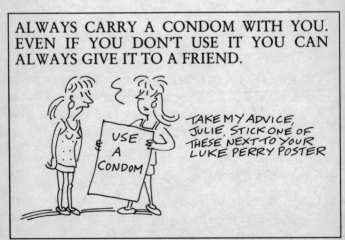

GLOSSARY

AIDS   Acquired Immune Deficiency Syndrome. For a more detailed explanation see p.38

ANAL INTERCOURSE   Sex in which a man puts his penis into another man's or woman's anus (bottom).

ANTIBODY POSITIVE   someone who IS carrying the HI virus.

ANTIBODY NEGATIVE   someone who is NOT carrying the HI virus.

ANTIBODIES   Chemicals developed by the body to fight infections.

ARC   AIDS Related Complex. A list of infections which are not serious enough to have an AIDS diagnosis but more severe than HIV. A sign that the virus is becoming active.

BISEXUAL   A person who enjoys sex with both men and women.

CONDOM   A thin rubber sheath put over the penis during sex to help protect against HIV and other sexual diseases and pregnancy (a condom is also called a rubber, Durex, johnny, trojan).

EPIDEMIC   An attack of a disease affecting lots of people across lots of countries.

GAY   A man or woman who has sex only with someone of their own sex ie man with man, woman with woman.

GENITALIA   The external (the bits you can see) sex organs. In a woman it's the vulva, including the labia (inner and outer lips) and the clitoris. In a man it's the penis, scrotum and testicles.

GUM CLINIC   Genito Urinary Medicine Clinic.

HETEROSEXUAL   A person that has sexual partners of the opposite sex to themselves. Man to woman, woman to man.

HIV   Human Immuno Deficiency Virus.

HOMOSEXUAL   A person who has sexual partners of the same sex as themselves ie a man with a man, a woman with a woman. The more common words used are gay for guys, and lesbian for women. Lesbian women sometimes call themselves gay as well.

HTLV-3 Human T cell Lymphotropic Virus Type 3 the name researchers first gave the HI virus.

IMMUNITY   The body's ability to fight infection.

LESBIAN   A women who has sex only with other women.

OPPORTUNISTIC INFECTIONS   An infection that enters the body and takes hold when the body is vulnerable and weak. In this case when the fighter cells have been destroyed by the HI virus.

PANDEMIC   An attack of a disease affecting millions of people across the world.

PCP   Pneumocystis carinii pneumonia, an opportunistic infection that settles in the lungs.

PENETRATIVE INTERCOURSE   Sex in which the penis enters the vagina (woman's sex organs) or anus (bottom).

PERIOD   Also called menstruation. The female body spends around a month preparing itself for a pregnancy. If the egg it releases isn't fertilised by a sperm it gets rid of all the 'preparation' (blood, tissue etc. from the womb) This comes out through the vagina once a month and is commonly known as a period, 'time of the month', the curse, being 'on'.

SEMEN   Fluid, containing sperm, ejaculated from a man's penis (also called cum or spunk)

SEXUAL ABUSE: When a person is forced to have sex without their consent. If you find yourself in this situation remember you're not alone.
Tell someone you trust or ring
CHILDLINE on   0800 1111
or SURVIVORS on   071 833 3737
You won't get into trouble.

STD   Sexually Transmitted Disease: infections passed from one person to another by having sex.

VACCINE   Medical treatment given by injection to boost immunity to other germs.

VAGINAL INTERCOURSE   Sex in which the penis enters the vagina.

VIRUS   A germ which can cause infection and can multiply inside the cells of the body.

★ FREE ★   ★ FREE ★   ★ FREE ★

There are lots of leaflets you can get free:

HIV/AIDS: The facts you need to know
There's a good basic leaflet available from the Health Education Authority in 8 different languages with equivalent English translations.
The languages so far are: Afro-Caribbean, Arabic, Bengali, Cantonese, Gujarati, Punjabi, Swahili and Urdu.

Welsh: The Cardiff AIDS helpline 0222 223443 have Welsh speakers and will tell you where to get leaflets written in Welsh. Ring for details.

There are loads more – for details on all sorts of information packs, booklets, videos, helplines, specialist support groups and lots more check out the list below.

LIST OF ORGANISATIONS

AIDS INFORMATION SERVICE (24 hrs)   0800 555 777
Free phoneline provides information and
sends free leaflets

AVERT   0403 210202
AIDS Education and Research Trust
11 Denne Parade
Horsham
West Sussex RH12 1JD
Publishes a range of information on the
subject. Some free leaflets.

BODY POSITIVE   071 835 1045
51B Philbeach Gardens
London SW5 9EB
A brilliant centre run for and by people
who are HIV+. They have centres all
round the country and will tell you your
local group. They provide help, literature,
great lunches and advice and they're
always needing volunteers.

BROOK ADVISORY CENTRE   071 708 1234
153a East St
London SE17 2SD
Contraception and counselling service
for young people. Friendly and accessible.
Free condoms. Ring for details of your
local centre or look in local phone book
under Brook or Family Planning.

Brook
ADVISORY CENTRES

BLACKLINERS
PO Box 74
London SW12 9JY
Information, leaflets and advice for black
people who are HIV positive.

BHAN   081 742 9223 –
Black HIV AIDS Network   helpline
111 Devonport Rd,   081 749 2828 –
London W12 8PB   admin
National organisation providing services
for Asian, African and Afro-Caribbean
people.

CARA (care and resources for people   071 792 8299
affected by HIV/AIDS)
The Basement
178 Lancaster Road
London W11 1QU
Provide services to people affected by
HIV/AIDS including funeral and bereave-
ment services, pastoral care, counselling
and other personal services. Offers
education and training courses about
issues of AIDS from a non-judgmental
perspective.

Catholic Aids Link   071 250 1394

CHILDLINE   0800 1111
Freepost 1111
London N1 0BR

The free national telephone helpline for children in trouble or danger. ChildLine provides a confidential counselling service for any child with any problem, 24 hours a day, every day.

CRUSAID   071 834 7566
Walcott St
London NW1
Crusaid have loads of great gifts and products. They'll also suggest lots of ideas for fundraising events. Ring or write to Jane for details.

Department of Education   081 533 2000

Department of Health   071 972 5275
AIDS Unit
80 London Road,
Elephant & Castle
London SE1

Directory of Social Change   071 435 8171
Radius Works
Back Lane
London NW3 1HL

Publishes lots of books about fundraising in connection with HIV/AIDS. Some free leaflets.

Dublin AIDS RESOURCE CENTRE   (01) 660 2149
Baggot Street Clinic
19 Haddington Rd
Dublin
Opening times; Tuesday 2.30–5pm, Wednesday 5–7pm, Thursday 5–7pm Offers advice/support re HIV/AIDS. HIV testing.

Family Planning Association   071 636 7866
27/35 Mortimer St
London W1N 7RJ
Offers information and advice on contraception and sexual health. Free leaflets available from the confidential helpline, Monday to Friday 10–3, which can also give you the address of your local family planning clinic. Hundreds of other publications available on sexuality, relationships and sexual health from the Healthwise bookshop and mail order service: catalogue free on request.

FPA
FAMILY PLANNING
A S S O C I A T I O N

Family Planning Association Wales   0222 342766
4 Museum Place
Cardiff CF1 3BG

Family Planning Association Northern   0232 325 488
Ireland
113 University St
Belfast BT7 1HP

The Gill and Mark Story   071 272 5958
c/o Susanna Dawson
PO Box 7
London W3 6XJ

For copies of the book, video, teacher's pack or home users pack. Information on the project and address to send donations.

GUM Clinic
Ring the National AIDS helpline (0800 567123) for the telephone number and address of your local GUM clinic.

HAEMOPHILIA SOCIETY   071 928 2020
123 Westminster Bridge Rd
London SE21 7HR

Advice, information and leaflets on haemophilia, and haemophilia with HIV/AIDS.

HEA Health Education Authority   071 383 3833
Hamilton House
Mabledon Place
London WC1H 9TX

They publish a wide range of material on HIV and sexual health. Free leaflets and information.

Lesbian and Gay Switchboard   071 837 7324
BM Switchboard
London WC1N 3XX
Advice, information and support for people who are gay or who think they may be.

LONDON LIGHTHOUSE   071 792 1200
111/7 Lancaster Rd
London W11 1QT

Drop-in centre and residential unit offering a range of services for people living with or affected by HIV/AIDS. Always looking for volunteers.

NAMES PROJECT UK
797 Christchurch Rd
Boscombe Bournemouth
Dorset BH 7 6AW
Produces the quilt in memory of those
who have died.

NATIONAL AIDS HELPLINE (24hrs)   0800 567 123
Confidential information and advice ab-
out all aspects of HIV/AIDS. 24 hours a
day, every day.

They also provide taped information   0800 622 509

For people with a hearing impairment   0800 521 361
10am – 10pm daily (counsellor)

Speaking Chinese (Cantonese)   0800 282 446
6–10pm Tuesdays (counsellor)

24 hr taped info in Cantonese   0800 622 506

Speaking Arabic   0800 282 447
6–10pm Wednesdays (counsellor)

24 hr taped information in Arabic   0800 622 507

African and Caribbean Backgrounds   0800 567 123
6–10pm Fridays (counsellor)

Speaking Bengali, Gujarati, Hindi, Punjabi,   0800 282 445
Urdu
6–10pm Wednesdays (counsellor)
24hr taped info in Bengali (Silheti dialect)   0800 622 501
24hr taped info in Gujarati   0800 622 503
24hr taped info in Hindi   0800 622 502
24hr taped info in Punjabi   0800 622 504
24hr taped info in Urdu   0800 622 505

THE NATIONAL AIDS HELPLINE
WILL KNOW EVERY GROUP ROUND
THE COUNTRY, AS WELL AS GUM
CLINICS AND FPA's.

NATIONAL AIDS TRUST (NAT)   071 972 2845
6th Floor Euston House
80 Newington Causeway
London SE1 6EF
The NAT organise World AIDS Day on
December 1st each year and have leaflets
and information on their various works
and projects. They're very helpful.

NHPIS   071 724 7993
National HIV Prevention Information
Service
82/86 Seymour Place
London W1H 5DB
Free national information service provid-
ing press cuttings, latest developments,
statistics etc. (9–5pm Mon–Fri)

Northern Ireland AIDS Helpline   0232 326117
operates on Monday, Wednesday and   7.30–10pm
      Friday
      Saturday   2.00–5pm

NSPCC Helpline (free)   0800 181118
Advice, information and referrals. 24
hours.

PARENTS ENQUIRY
16 Homley Rd
Catford
London SE26 2HZ
Help for parents of young lesbians and gay
men.

City and Hackney Young People's Project 071 601 7100
Rm 301 St Leonards Hospital
Nuttall Street
London N1 5LZ

Positively Irish Action on AIDS 081 983 0192

POSITIVELY WOMEN
5 Sebastian St
London EC1V 0HE
Provides support advice and leaflets for women affected by HIV.

POSITIVE YOUTH 071 373 7547
51B Philbeach Gardens
London SW5 9EB
For young people concerned about HIV.

RAPE CRISIS CENTRE 071 278 3956
PO Box 69 information and
London WC1X 9NJ leaflets

071 837 1600
24hr helpline

Red Ribbon International 071 935 5996
32 James St
London W1M 5HS
Red Ribbon International's fundamental objective is to encourage the development of the Red Ribbon symbol. The symbol represents a united international HIV/AIDS awareness showing care and understanding towards people who live and have lived with HIV/AIDS. They provide red ribbons and merchandise on a large scale.

RED RIBBON INTERNATIONAL

The St Stephens AIDS Research Appeal   081 746 5592
London House
226 Fulham Rd
London SW109EL
They produce brilliant T shirts with a
colour-changing condom on the front for
£10.00 + p&p.
All proceeds go to research.

SAMARITANS   071 439 2224
Available 24 hours a day, every day of the
year, to befriend the despairing and
suicidal.
Look in the telephone book for your local
number.

SAM
Scottish AIDS information line
PO Box 48
Edinburgh EH1 5SA
Information, advice and support on HIV/
AIDS. Will also know local groups.

SCODA – Standing Conference on Drug   071 430 2341
Abuse
1/4 Hatton Place
Hatton Garden
London EC1N 8ND

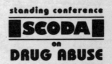

The national coordinating and repre-
sentative body for drug services and
those working with drug users. Bi-
monthly newsletter, directories and
county lists of services as well as needle
exchange lists and HIV and drugs booklet.

TERENCE HIGGINS TRUST   (admin)   071 831 0330
52/54 Grays Inn Rd   (helpline 3–10pm)   071 242 1010
London WC1X 8JU
A registered charity to inform, advise and help on AIDS and HIV infection. Also runs volunteer and buddy groups.

BRITISH YOUTH COUNCIL   071 387 7559
57 Charlton St
London NW1 1HU
Umbrella body for young people's organisations covering people aged 16–25. Its primary aim is to advance the interest and views of young people and to enable young people to play a more active part in all aspects of political and public decision making.

YOUTH CLUBS UK   071 353 2366
11 St Bride Street
London WC4A 4AS
Umbrella organisation for youth clubs nationwide. Run a series of Health Fairs in conjunction with The Health Authority, dealing with issues such as sexual health, alcohol and drug abuse and currently have preventative peer education on this subject in several areas throughout the country. Produce a bi-monthly magazine 'Youth Clubs'.

YOUTH ENQUIRY SERVICE   041 227 6800
155 Bath Street
Glasgow G2 2SQ
Provides advice, information and referral to counselling agencies for young people and youth workers.